Both of Em'

A Fictional Erotica Romance Novel

Both Of Em':

Volume 1

Written by:

Nina Monroe

Moe Nicole

AUTHOR ENTREPRENEUR CONTENT CURATOR

This book is a work of fiction.

Published by *Live out Loud Press*

An Imprint of Moe Nicole

ISBN-13: 978-1-7340606-5-2

www.MoeNicole.com

We live in a world

That loves to make us feel

as if our desires are too much.

What if you could cultivate the romantic life you really wanted?

CHAPTERS

Contents

BOTH OF EM':
Volume 1

Whew Chile, So lemme tell you how all of this started....

Chapter 1: Well look at that

Trina sat looking at the boxes sitting in the middle of the living room floor, that were meant to be used to pack up the rest of the items in her kitchen. All she could do was look with a blank face as her right leg shook at an increasing rate. Here she was, uprooting her entire life once again and moving to cold ass Michigan. She had just moved back to San Francisco after living in Phoenix for two years. Prior to that she was in the mid-south working on her degree in Memphis. Just when she thought she was preparing to settle back in her home city, she was given an offer that would make her a fool to decline.

A month prior, Trina attended the Advocates of Education annual summit in Louisville, Kentucky. She wasn't supposed to attend at first, but her partner had gotten sick and the company needed someone to go in her place at the last minute. A conference was the last thing on her mind, as all she was praying for was a vacation and some dick. Well, that's if she got lucky and finally found the time to meet someone with one. But here she was, still working.

Her company, Altech, was going through an internal structural change and the conference was supposed to be used as a way to build new relationships and connections with other companies and institutions that were working for educational equity. Although Altech wasn't an educational institution, they were heavily involved in the distribution of educational materials and textbooks. This meant that Trina needed to be attentive of who was in the room at all times. Because in the world of contracts, you have to always know what your potential customers need.

Before leaving the office to head to the airport, her Boss Sharon passed her the conference itinerary of each session with different ones marked with a red asterisk. Trina looked up at her with a questioning face, and automatically knew what was going on when she locked eyes with Sharon.

"I need you to connect with the presenter of these sessions," she said to Trina immediately, knowing what she was thinking.

"And what else do I need to know about the connections?" Trina asked hesitantly.

"Just find a way to get the information for their leaders, who are over the adoption of educational materials, before you fly back to San Fran. It's our plan to pitch to each institution to secure a certain level of funding for our upcoming projects," Sharon responded.

"Ok, cool," Trina said as she turned to head towards the door.

Stopping Trina in her tracks, Sharon shouted out "Don't mess this up Stansby, we really need this. It will help you with that promotion we talked about."

That statement slightly confused Trina, because they hadn't talked about a promotion. Instead of asking questions she decided to just shake it off and continued out the door while nodding in approval. It was a surprise her disdain didn't show.

But Sharon didn't stop her and she didn't look back either.

Trina made it to the airport about an hour prior to take-off, with traffic being the culprit. Her driver decided it was a smart idea to drive through San Fran's i80 traffic, like it was a Sunday morning. There were two accidents in a 1 mile radius that they were forced to wait through. Thankfully, the accidents didn't look like they were fatal. People needed to learn how to be more thoughtful and careful while driving in the city. There was always an active accident sweep on i80, which is why she avoided it most times. So much can happen in a blink of an eye and All Trina could think about was the last car accident she was in. She was minding her business and from out of nowhere, someone tried to cut in front of her and clipped the front of her bumper, forcing her car to spin in the middle of the freeway.

She was thankful to be alive.

Thankfully, she packed a carry-on bag and didn't have to worry about checking a bag, nor did she have to stand in the regular security line because she had Pre-Check services and her tickets saved on her phone.

There are some things we have to love about technology, Trina thought to herself as she stood in the short line.

It took a total of about 10 minutes for her to go through the security line and make-it to her gate. They hadn't started boarding yet, so she still had time to grab a snack to eat and book to read on the plane from the store next to the gate.

As she was browsing through the books available in the bookstore, she noticed a magazine on the shelf that featured a group of black men at the beach.

Her vagina instantly got wet as she started thinking about the last time she had sex. It had been a while and she was hesitant to do it again, even though she was hornier than a stray dog in heat. Her and her ex had been broken up for almost 9 months and she was still masturbating to the videos they made on her phone. Shit was getting old and she was missing the feeling of a warm hard body and dick in her mouth.

Trina bit her lip and put the magazine back on the shelf as she continued browsing through the books.

She locked eyes on the book Nia Bluu and knew she had to get a copy. Her friend had just told her about how much she loved it. She grabbed a copy of the book and a cup of fresh fruit from the refrigerator before heading to the register to check out.

As she stood in line waiting to be helped, she looked dead at the magazine again and started getting thoughts in her head of things she'd really like to be doing instead of flying to a work trip.

By the time she finished checking out, her plane was boarding business class. One thing about Trina, when she flew, she flew in style and that was always business class. She loved the extra room, free drinks and food, and the flight attendants were nicer.

The plane ride wasn't too bad as she made it to her layover in Chicago. She had an hour layover before she took her next flight into Louisville, so she decided to go for a walk while she waited. The airport was a decent size, but she was on a mission to eat once she got close to the food court. The smell of the chili cheese coneys had her mouth watering and stomach singing a joyful tune that she couldn't deny.

She decided to try out Eden's Deli, because their food smelled irresistible as she walked past. She tried to ignore it, but she couldn't. As she stood in line, she looked at the menu to solidify what she was going to order. When she finished deciding on what she was going to eat, she looked over her shoulder toward the restaurant next door and there was a handsome chocolate man staring at her with no remorse for being caught. They locked eyes at that moment.

Trina quickly turned her head and tried to look from the corner of her eye to see if he was still staring at her. She purposely made a point to not look his way again, even though she knew he was watching. He had piercing eyes that felt like they could command her soul with just the thoughts he possessed behind them.

Trina ordered her food and grabbed her drink before finding a seat in the court while she waited for her food.

As soon as she sat down, that same young man appeared next to her table as if he was waiting for her to take a seat.

"Do you mind if I join you?" He asked respectfully.

Trina couldn't help but notice the bass in his voice that sounded as if it was trained by the thunderstorms at night. He could be as respectful as he wanted, but she was thinking some real disrespectful thoughts.

"No, it's fine you can. I don't plan on being here for long," she replied back while trying to avoid eye contact with him. It felt like a set-up.

He sat his food on the table and then laid his suitcase next to the chair across from Trina and proceeded to take off his suit jacket, laid it on the chair next to him, and started taking a seat while rolling up his sleeves.

As much as Trina was trying to avoid eye contact, she couldn't help but notice how good he smelled and how his presence commanded her attention no matter how much she tried to hide it.

He had to be about 6'5" and 235 pounds. He looked like he had alot of muscle mass and was a faithful goer to the sex traphouse, also known as the Gym.

"My name is Damon Sylvestian, and yours?" He asked while reaching his hand out for a handshake.

"My name is Trina," she responded while hesitantly shaking his hand. As soon as their hands met, he gave her a slight grip and moved his hand slowly while scaling every last inch of her middle finger.

Trina instantly got wet and started thinking about knowing more about Damon. Honestly, at this point she didn't care about his name. She just wanted to see what his mouth do.

"So, I gave you my full name, I can't get yours?" He asked jokingly while pulling out his silver ware.

"Well, Mr. Sylvestian, I don't know you like that so my first name is good enough," she shot back defensively.

"Oh, don't worry Ms. Trina, I don't mean to make you defensive, I was simply making an observation," He added while taking a bite of his caesar salad.

"So where are you flying to?" Trina asked.

"Oh, you waste no time in getting to the nitty gritty I see," He said in a joking manner.

"I'm just trying to make conversation with a stranger that asked to sit next to me," Trina responded.

"You know, it's something about that feistiness that really turns me on," Damon said with a smooth voice and corner smile.

Trina started blushing uncontrollably, as she didn't expect for him to feel what she was feeling.

"What about it turns you on?" She asked.

"It tells me that you know how to take care of yourself and control situations when it's needed," he said.

"Looks like you've been doing your homework," Trina said with a laugh.

"Nah, I can just tell when I come across a real woman." Damon said with a straight face.

Trina cleared her throat as the waiter brought her food and sat it on the table.

"Soooo, back to the question, where are you headed? It looks like you're either leaving work or headed to do some work" she asked as she looked him up and down with his tailored suit.

"Very observant, I like that," Damon responded. "I'm headed to a conference in Louisville for my job.

Trina's mouth and vagina got wetter as she thought about the fact they may be attending the same conference.

She wasn't going to tell him that though.

Chapter 2: There is a gawd

Damon looked at Trina waiting for her to share where she was going, but she quickly changed the topic.

"So, what type of work do you do?" She asked.

"I guess that's something you are going to have to wonder about, since we are choosing to keep information from each other" Damon responded in a stern voice with one eyebrow raised.

Trina giggled and started preparing her food. "You're cute, I like that."

Damon adjusted in his seat and took another bite of his salad.

As he bit down on his food, Trina finished packing her food to go.

"I enjoyed this chat Sir," she said while standing and turning. "I hope you have a safe flight headed to your destination. I need to get to my gate. Enjoy the rest of your food and day."

He wiped the salad dressing from the side of his mouth and took a big swallow as the rest of the food disappeared in his mouth.

"I enjoyed the chat with you as well Ms. Lady. Maybe we will have the opportunity of seeing each other again," He said with a smile.

"Same," Trina said as she turned to walk away.

"Wait, wait, hold up Ms. Trina!" Damon said loudly as Trina started to walk away. "Can I have your phone number? I'd love to stay in contact with you."

"Some encounters are best enjoyed in the moment instead of hoping for the next," Trina said with a smile and walked away.

Damon looked at her slightly confused at what had just happened.

Trina didn't know if he was going to call after her or allow her to keep walking. Either way it went, she had a strong feeling that she was going to run into him when she got to Louisville.

When she made it back to the gate, she noticed that she still had a couple minutes before they would be boarding her group so she pulled out her phone and started surfing the web for conferences in Louisville.

In just 3 minutes, she was able to identify 3 other conferences that were going on at the same time in Louisville. It hit her that it was simply a fated encounter that was meant to happen and nothing more.

A part of her was upset that she didn't get his phone number.

A few minutes later, it was time for her to board the plane to her destination and all she could think about was making it to her hotel room and resting.

Her flight from Chicago was about an hour and a half long and smooth. As soon as she arrived at the baggage claim exit her driver was already there waiting for her, making it perfect timing.

The drive from the airport to the hotel was less than 10 miles which was perfect. She was staying at the Raiton Pelaton Downtown, across the street from the host hotel and couldn't wait to get to her accommodations.

The Raiton Pelaton had better rates and better room options available to suit her taste more. All she had to do was wake-up 5 minutes earlier, so she could make it across the street on time for the sessions to start every day.

She was able to get a room on the top floor of the hotel in the corner, facing the bridge. The sky was so beautiful as it reflected the faint stars and moon from the sky as the sun had finished setting.

I'm not closing these blinds the whole time I'm here, Trina thought to herself as she started taking off her clothes and walking towards the bathroom with her suitcase.

She started taking out all of her bathroom items from the suitcase and turned on the shower to clean off the day.

The bathroom was decorated delicately with an all glass shower and stone decorated tiles. Outside of the bathroom was a deep seated hot tub big enough to fit 5 people comfortably. It was surrounded by a canopy and plants that created a comfortable atmosphere. Trina was all for the natural beauty and vibe.

By the time she was out of the shower, it was darker outside and she was ready for bed. As soon as she made it to the bed, she instantly started thinking about Damon and how bad she would've loved having the opportunity to ride his face instead of laying in the bed alone. The shower mustn't have cleaned off all of the day because she was still feeling dirty! Well, thinking it at least.

Trina jumped out of the bed and grabbed a silk satchel out of her suitcase that housed her rose toy. She jumped in the bed, unwrapped the towel from her body and started visualizing Damon, naked in front of her.

As she thought about what it would feel like having him giving her oral, she rubbed the rose on her clit faster as the vibrations and suction increased. She moaned uncontrollably as her clit throbbed to the vibrations of her toy and the vision of Damon looking up at her as he took her soul. Next thing she knew, he was hitting her from the back while choking her passionately.

Not long after, she was cumming and couldn't stop shaking.

She had to have him.

Trina was awakened by the sunrise peering through the windows on the east side of the room. Today was the day for the conference registration and opening ceremony that started at 5 that evening.

Since registration started at 8am, she wanted to go early to beat the afternoon rush that was bound to happen. Most people fly into conferences right before the opening ceremonies, it's a known fact. On top of that, it was a Wednesday, so she was confident in her predictions.

It was about 7 o'clock, which gave her plenty of time to unpack her suitcase, get dressed, head to registration and then breakfast. She had it all planned out.

Out of nowhere, her phone started ringing, and she knew it couldn't be anyone else but Kisha. Kisha is Trina's best friend of 20 years. They found out they were dating the same guy freshman year of high school and decided to set him up. After they completed that mission, they became inseparable.

Trina answered the phone, "Hey girl, why are you up so early?"

"Girlllll, I had to make sure you had a plan in order for the dick mission!" Kisha shot back.

Trina burst out laughing! "Girl, I am here to work, not focus on getting dick," She responded while walking across the room back to the window.

"I mean, we know that, but we also know that you haven't had any in a long time and the best kind of dick is the kind that happens away from home" Kisha said enthusiastically.

Trina looked around the room. She knew she agreed with Kisha, but she didn't want to give her the benefit of the doubt.

"You remember our trip to New Orleans? Babyyyy, that was a good ass time!" Kisha said.

Trina immediately started biting her bottom lip and dazing off into the ceiling as she thought about the one-night stand that gave her magical powers.

"Trina!" Kisha yelled.

"Oh, my bad girl. I had a flashback," she said with a giggle. "I'm not going to lie, there was a man I met at the airport in Chicago who is in Louisville right now for work. I should've got his number, cause he definitely looked like a ride I wanted a ticket to."

"You are always out here messing up the vibe. But hey, there are other dicks in the sea" Kisha responded.

"Alright, so you remember the rules. No sex in your room unless it's the last night. Get their first and last name, with a picture of id at all times... alot of these men are crazy. Oh yea, always meet in a public place first!" Kisha said, sounding like a mama.

"Girl, you know I know the rules and I already packed protection. I have no time to be getting caught up hunny," Trina responded.

"You throwing shade, or nah?" Kisha asked with a laugh.

"If the shoe fits, I already know you're going to wear it proud," Trina laughed back. "Let me go in here and get my life together before it gets busy."

"No problem my love. May the dick be with you!" Kisha said with excitement.

They both hung up the phone giggling. Trina loved the relationship her and Kisha had. Whenever one of them were going through something, they could count on the other to come and be a major support.

When Kisha got pregnant during their trip to Jamaica a couple of years ago, it sent her into a slight spiral and Trina was there every step of the way helping her through it. Here it was 2 years later and her and her one night stand are now happily married as husband and wife.

It's interesting how life works.

It took Trina about 50 minutes to shower, put on a simple makeup look, and get dressed. She was able to make it to the registration counter right when they finished setting up the tables.

As she was completing the check-in process she looked to her right, in search of food, and there he was. Standing tall, strong, and handsome Damon was in her eyesight again. In the manner of 2 seconds, she felt her Vagina get wetter than the bottle of water she was holding in her hand.

He was there. It was meant.

Chapter 3: Just what I needed

She tried her best to play it cool. She put her registration items in her bag and turned around slowly to be met by him staring her directly in the face. Damon quickly bit his bottom lip and greeted Trina.

"Well look at what God blew my way today," He said with a grin while looking Trina up and down.

"Hello Damon," Trina said with a slight sigh and blushed grin. "Are you attending the Advocates of Education summit too?" She asked while turning to look at the registration table.

He laughed a little and replied, "yes I am."

Trina felt her entire body heating up from the chemistry they were putting into the atmosphere. She could tell he was feeling the same way she was by the way he kept biting his bottom lip and looking her body up and down after meeting her eyes with a piercing contact that looked like they were saying, "I want to fuck you."

She just knew that she was sending him the same signal too.

Trina felt her inner thighs start to sweat as the temperature of her vagina had reached ultimate heights. She had to have him.

"I was just headed to breakfast before getting the day started. Do you want to join me?" Trina asked him boldly. She usually waited for men to approach her first, but he technically did that already when he rolled up on her at the airport. She refused to lose contact with him again.

"That actually sounds like a great idea, because I was looking for food too," Damon responded while licking his lips and sizing Trina up and down.

Trina couldn't take it anymore and she needed to lose eye contact for a moment.

She looked around the foyer and suggested they go to the restaurant across the street at the other hotel.

"Is that where you're staying?" Damon asked.

"Why are you all in my business?" Trina responded passively.

"Well I'm letting you all in my business by telling you that's where I'm staying. If you cared to know," Damon responded.

"Well excuse me Mr. Politically Correct! I still need to make sure you're not a serial killer or anything." Trina responded with a nervous laugh as she began walking towards the door.

"Girl, you got a walk on you," Damon said with a slowed down tone.

They crossed the street and entered through the automatic doors to the hotel. When they got to the restaurant door, Damon jumped in front of Trina to open the door and let her in.

"Thank you," she said with a smile and head nod.

"It's really beautiful here, I love the ambience," Trina said as she looked around and made her way to the hostess stand to the right.

"Yea, they are setting the mood before I even had to try," Damon said with a laugh.

"Boy, what mood are you trying to set?" Trina asked with a smirk on her face.

"Any mood you want me to," he answered.

"See, you just want me for my goodies," Trina shot back.

"Hello, a seat for 2?" The hostess walked up asking.

"Yes please," Damon responded.

Whew, he knows how to take control, Trina thought to herself.

When they made it to the table, Damon asked Trina which side of the table she preferred to sit. He proceeded to take her jacket and pulled out her chair before placing her jacket on the chair next to them.

I'm sure I have a puddle under me, Trina thought to herself as she felt the moistness of her vagina soaking her panties.

The waitress left menus at the table for the pair and went to grab them glasses of water and coffee. While the waitress was gone, they both looked at the menu for their order.

It didn't take long for Trina to find what she wanted to order. They had a seafood omelet on the menu that sounded like it would be good. When she finished identifying what she wanted to order, she looked up at Damon to see if he was still choosing. To her surprise, he was looking at her.

"Damn, why are you staring at me like I'm your breakfast?" Trina laughed.

"I mean, I would prefer to be eating you, but I'm patient for what I want." Damon responded seriously.

Trina started squirming in her seat at the sound of his rumbling voice. *Did this man just say that he wished he was eating me?* She thought to herself. That turned her on tremendously.

"Well oh shit," she blurted out before disappearing into her purse, acting like she was looking for something.

"Uh huh" he responded while licking his lips.

Just as he finished, the waitress made her way back to the table with their water and coffee.

"Would you like sugar and cream?" She asked them both.

"I'll take hazelnut please," Trina said.

Damon raised his hand, "no thank you."

"Ma'am, I need to go to the back to grab some hazelnut creamer, I'll be back." The waitress said to Trina.

"Ok, no problem."

"I see you like your coffee black," Trina said to Damon.

"I Just have a thing for people and things in their natural state," He said before sitting up in his chair and taking a sip of his black coffee without a flinch of dissatisfaction in his face.

"So tell me a little about yourself," Trina said to Damon, changing the conversation.

"Well, I work in education administration at a school district in Michigan. I like to travel. I don't have any kids, I-"

"Oh dang, you don't have any baby mamas I have to worry about? That's no fun!" Trina interrupted sarcastically.

"You are a mess. Do you have any children?" He asked.

"No, I don't have any children. I have all the respect in the world for people with children though," she answered.

"You don't have to tell me that twice," Damon responded.

When the waitress returned to the table with the hazelnut creamers, they both ordered their food. Trina ordered the seafood omelet and Damon ordered the Chicken and Waffles with shrimp with grits.

"Sorry for interrupting, you can continue," Trina said as she mixed her coffee.

"Oh it's ok, beautiful. You can interrupt me anytime."

They both laughed.

"I'm the oldest child, 38 years old, and my favorite color is blue," he laughed. "And you?"

"I'm a purple kind of girl, am 33 years old, starting to hate my job, the oldest child as well, and am into all things creative," she responded.

"Why do you hate your job? What do you do?" He asked.

"I work for a major educational textbook publishing company as the outreach manager, that's about all I really want to talk about right now" she finished.

"Oh I definitely understand. We have plenty of time to discuss work. Right now, I want to know the intimate parts of yourself that you don't tell everyone," he said convincingly.

Once they started talking, time flew. Over the course of 20 minutes, they found themselves laughing, smiling, talking about the future, flirting, and horny as hell.

When the food came, it didn't take long for it to disappear in their stomachs. They both had a long day of traveling the day before. Not only did they get a delicious meal, they hit it off in a special kind of way.

"I definitely need a nap after that," Damon said leaning back and rubbing his belly.

"Me too," Trina said while fighting an incoming yawn.

"It would be better if you were taking a nap with me," he responded.

As soon as he finished talking, the waitress brought the bill back to the table. Without hesitation, Damon grabbed the bill and Trina let out a thank you while reaching for her purse.

"I'll get the tip," she said.

"No ma'am, put that back in your purse," He shot back while pulling out his bank card. The waitress took the bill to process the payment and Damon looked at Trina.

"I want you Trina. I want you in a serious way. Now, if you don't want me to, I understand. But I feel like I need to taste you."

Trina couldn't bring herself to respond. She just looked at him until the waitress returned with the receipt.

When Damon finished signing the bill, he got up and grabbed Trina's jacket off the chair. He walked over to her seat and placed his hand on her shoulder before pulling out her chair.

Trina rolled her neck as she envisioned him with his hands around her neck.

Trina knew what time it was. So did Damon.

Chapter 4: Feeling like a prize, hunty!

It didn't take long for them to reach the elevators. As soon as they pressed the button, the elevator on the right was opening. They quickly jumped on and pressed the close button. Damon pressed the 11th floor and then turned and started kissing Trina with no warning.

He took his right hand and slid it under her dress and started playing with her clitoris making her moan from the stimulation. Trina was beyond wet, to the point she knew his hand would come out full of her juices. He pulled his fingers out and put them in his mouth to taste her.

"You taste like nectar," he said in a low sexy tone. He proceeded to lick it all off his finger, "I can't wait to have you," He said.

Trina pressed her face on his and they started kissing uncontrollably, until the elevator reached the 11th floor.

"I want you to carry me," Trina said jokingly.

Damon didn't get the hint of it being a joke, because he picked Trina up and put her over his shoulders as he walked to his room like superman.

When he made it in the room, he laid Trina on the bed and they didn't waste any time before ripping each other's clothes off. Trina took off Damon's shirt and he pulled her dress up over her head before laying her back on the bed.

"I just want to take a moment and look at you," He said as his eyes glazed over her body. "You are so beautiful," He stated as he started taking off her shoes and then panties that were under her dress. He then proceeded to kiss Trina on her neck and made his way down to her belly button. He licked and kissed around her belly button while one of his hands fondled one of her nipples as the other played with her clit with one finger penetrating in and out.

Damon's masculine energy was gleaming through his voice, his body, and his kisses. They both craved each other in a deep way. It had been so long since Trina had sex, so she was slightly worried, but she was excited even more.

Would he be too big? Would he be hard or gentle? She thought to herself as he pleasured her in more than one way.

Eventually, she couldn't control it and as she was on the verge of cumming he stopped kissing her belly and made his way down to her clit. As he kissed her clit, he had his hand squeezing her other nipple to the same pace as the suctioning of his mouth on her clit. He sucked her clit gently, taking moments to lick inside her lips, slurping up all the wetness. He made his way back to her clit and stuck his finger inside her vagina. As he penetrated her vagina with his finger he sucked on her clit faster and faster.

In a matter of seconds, Trina was cumming all over Damon's face. He was taking her soul as he didn't stop sucking. As she came, he penetrated her vagina faster and faster, stimulating her g-spot in a way it had never been stimulated before.

"Oh baby, I want to feel you. Please?" Trina begged.

He didn't answer. He kept sucking and penetrating her vagina. It was getting hard for Trina to control it as he sucked on her clit in the perfect way. Next thing she knew, she was squirting all over his face. He was soaked and smiling.

"That's a good girl," he said as he came up with a smile on his face. He was smiling like it was his favorite pastime and he had just arisen from a river.

"That's a good girl. You like how daddy did that?" He asked Trina

Without hesitation, she responded, "Yes daddy."

"What do you want daddy to do next for his woman?"

"I want to feel you."

"Are you sure you're ready?" He asked.

Trina hadn't seen his penis yet, because they hadn't gotten that far, but honestly it wasn't that she really cared.

At this point, Trina just wanted to be set free from her long drought. She was ok with being fucked hard, soft, whatever. All she knew was that she wanted to be taken to ecstasy. She wanted her Damon daddy to set her free.

He started playing with her clit again as she told him she wanted him. His finger went deeper and deeper, tapping her g-spot. Trina's body started jerking as she tried to control the pleasure he was giving her. It was getting hard, just like his dick that she was starting to feel on her leg.

"You ready to receive me baby?" He asked with a deepened voice.

"I've been ready, baby." She responded as she made her way off her back. She turned his body and got on top of him as she kissed his neck. She licked from his ear down to his breast, pulling his pants down as she went further and further. As she made her way to his belly, she took her hand and started rubbing his penis; clutching his balls at the same time.

It was thick and had to be at least 7 inches of hard wood.

This turned Damon on in so many ways, to the point he demanded she stop.

"Baby, I want to please you some more," he said. " I love the reaction you have to me when you're cumming. I'm addicted."

He wanted to see if he could make her cum again. As much as Trina wanted the dick, she loved the way he sucked her clit too. He flipped her over so fast and the control was his once again. This time, he grabbed both her wrists and held them there and he sucked passionately on her clit. Trina sat up and watched him suck on her, while he penetrated her vagina with his fingers.

Next thing she knew, she was cumming again, but it was much more intense. Her body started shaking uncontrollably as she squirted all over his face again. He started licking her juices off his lips as he raised his head with a big smile on his face once again. You would think he had won the lottery.

"I love when you shower my face!" He said with his grin getting bigger.

Trina sat there slightly embarrassed because that was the first time she had squirted with someone during oral sex before. It was something about the intensity they shared that turned her on drastically and increased her body heat.

If that's what his tongue did, she was scared to see exactly what his dick would do inside of her. Damon had a sex appeal that not many men had in Trina's eyes. From just looking at him, her vagina got juicy. She didn't know what it was about him, but she did know that she wanted to fuck him. She wanted to ride his dick until she couldn't ride it anymore.

"Let me grab a condom from my bag," Trina said to Damon as she sat up on the bed preparing herself for the King that was in front of her.

He looked at her and asked, "Are you sure? I swear I'm clean. I haven't had sex since my divorce."

"Divorce?" Trina asked with surprise.

"Yes divorce. It's been final for 6 months and I haven't had intercourse in almost 12," he responded.

"Unprotected sex with you would have me addicted and pregnant," Trina said.

"I promise I'll pull out," he said. "I just want to feel all of you, baby. It's something about you that I can't explain."

Trina reached over to her bag and pulled out a condom, handing it to him.

Damon took the condom without a word, opened it, and rolled it over his delicious looking human snicker bar. Trina could tell he wasn't happy, but she wasn't willing to risk it the first time meeting him. She still wanted the dick though.

Damon crawled on the bed, towards Trina and laid her back.

"I want you to relax for daddy, ok," he calmly said as he kissed her neck while inserting his manhood.

Trina took a deep breath in. She was in ecstasy.

They made love for over an hour. From the bed, to the window ledge, to the bathroom counter; they christened every part of the hotel room with their juices and sweat. It was when he had Trina bent over the couch when Damon could no longer maintain himself. He had held out for over an hour and the pressure had built up to a place of no return.

"Oh Queen, your King is cumming," he trembled to say.

Trina purposefully squeezed her vagina tighter. Gripping every inch as he pushed in and out of her. She felt the intensity rise; his pulsing penis was ready to explode.

"I want you to cum for me King. Let it all out for Mama," Trina said softly.

Next thing she knew, he exploded and fell on top of her. He laid there for a good 20 seconds shaking and kissing the black of her neck, in an attempt to get his energy replenished, before rolling over.

"That was AMAZING!" Damon exclaimed while letting out a deep sigh.

"Too bad we stay worlds apart," Trina laughed.

"I mean, it doesn't have to be that way. Finding you a new job wouldn't be a problem. I mean, I am over the school district of a major city," Damon responded.

"OVER a school district?" Trina asked with her eyebrow raised. "You said administrator, you didn't say anything about being over something."

"Some things are better left unsaid," he responded.

"Well, we will leave that to be a problem for tomorrow. We both need to get ready for this opening ceremony later today," Nikki responded.

"Is that your way of telling me you're about to leave?" He asked. "You're just going to hit it and quit it huh?" He laughed.

That was exactly what Trina had planned to do. She was in no position to be catching feelings for a man that she had just met and decided to fuck. Life was a little more complicated than that. Cuddling would only intensify the moment and she wasn't ready for that reality.

"We just have a busy day ahead of us, and I don't want to be a distraction," Trina responded.

"Well what if I want you to distract me?" He asked while pulling himself closer to her again.

She thought about it for a moment. All she could think about was his divorce.

"You're recently divorced. I can't forget that." She said.

"I promise that wasn't my fault. I caught her cheating with my bestfriend. I couldn't look at either one of them the same after that happened." Damon said with a lowered tone.

He turned his head and looked out the window.

"The thing is, this was fun for the moment. But I want to treat it for what it was. I don't want to get attached to an emotionally unavailable man," Trina said as she pulled away from him to get up.

"You can trust me when I say that I want to be married again. There's something special about you and I want to dive into all of you," he responded.

By this time, Trina was putting on her panties, while looking around for her dress.

"It's right there on the floor by the couch," Damon said as he got up from the bed to grab it for her.

After retrieving her dress he made his way towards her, while ruffling the dress to put over her head. "Do you have anything to say to that?" He asked while putting her dress on.

"I want to be married too, but you live all the way in Michigan and I live all the way in California."

"Well at least let's exchange numbers and start communicating. We don't have to talk about our future together. I just don't want to lose contact with you," he pleaded.

Trina grabbed her phone out of her purse and opened her text messages. There was a message from Kisha. *Wait until she hears about this shit,* Trina thought to herself.

"What's your phone number?" She asked while composing a new message.

"313-555-2137," he said.

"I just texted you. You can reach me at that number," she said as she put on her shoes and made her way to the door.

Damon ran behind her to meet her just as she turned the knob to open it. "Can I at least have a kiss?"

Trina kissed him on his cheek and turned around to leave the room. She left him standing there, wanting and craving more. She didn't care one bit.

Chapter 5: Oh ok…

It didn't take long for her to make it to the elevator to head up to her room on the 18th floor. Next thing she knew, she was in the bathroom naked with the shower running.

I really just did that, she thought to herself as she looked in the mirror touching her face. "I really just fucked this random man, that just so happens to be over a school district," she said in the mirror.

I'm such a hoe, she thought as she turned to get into the shower.

She was in the shower for at least 15 minutes washing her body before getting out. She turned off the water, grabbed the towel from over the toilet and dried herself off before getting out. She wrapped the towel around her body as she stood in front of the mirror analyzing every inch of her exposed body.

"Shit happens," Trina said as she turned to walk into the main room area. She grabbed her phone to call Kisha, ready to gossip on the dick she just got.

As expected, Kisha answered the phone on the second ring.

"Heeeeey Girl, you miss me already?!" She yelled through the phone.

"Girrrrrrl, so that man I told you about…"

"Uh huh, the sexy man from the airport. What happened girl?" Kisha asked

"Sooooo, he is actually at the same conference as me and I just finished fucking him," Trina said while covering her mouth like she had just committed a top level sin.

"Well damn, that was fast. How was it?" Kisha asked while finding a seat in the corner of her living room.

"Girl, it was so damn good! I wish it didn't have to stop."

"Well why did it?" Kisha asked sarcastically.

"That man was about to dickmatize me and I don't have time for that," Trina laughed. "Plus, he's recently divorced girl. I don't."

"Girl, I do not care about all of that and neither should you." Kisha interrupted. "Here you go thinking extra deep about stuff once again, when there is nothing to worry about."

"It just felt like he was trying to move a little too fast with the things he was saying. I'm not used to that, Kisha. You know that," Trina said.

"Because of that, that may not be such a bad thing girl," Kisha said while taking a sip from her cup.

Trina was quiet for a moment, thinking about what Kisha had just said.

"Don't get quiet now," Kisha interrupted Trina's deep thinking.

"I mean you do have a point. I just don't know. We will see how the rest of the conference goes," Trina responded.

Zzzzz buzzed Trina's phone. She looked at the phone to see it was Damon messaging her.

Hey beautiful, did you make it fine? How are you feeling? His text read.

"What you reading? Cause I know you just got a text." Kisha demanded.

"And did," Trina said while smiling. *Yes, I made it in fine, just got out of the shower*, she responded to Damon.

"Girl, I'm about to let you go. I need to get this lunch together anyways. Go get you some more dick," Kisha giggled.

"Alright girl, I'mma hit you up later. Give my babies a kiss for me," Trina responded.

They both ended the call and Trina laid back on the bed. Next thing she knew, she was touching on her breast, thinking about Damon kissing her.

zzzzz Buzzed Trina's phone. It was another message from Damon.

We could've done that together

Trina looked at the message and laid her phone back down on the bed.

Let me get up and get ready for this conference, Trina thought to herself as she got off the bed. She spent a nice amount of time looking over her registration information, reading the presenter bios, and making a list of all the sessions she needed to attend. There were 4 sessions Sharon had marked for her to attend. Two of them were on Thursday and the other two were on Friday. This gave her time to look at two other sessions on both days.

As she skimmed through the sessions, she noticed that Damon had a session scheduled for Thursday morning, where he was presenting on *Using Social Media in the Education System to attract more students who are excited to learn*. Wanting to be nosey, she decided to plan on attending that session as well.

By the time she finished looking over the registration information it was time to get ready for the opening ceremony that started at 5. She spent the next hour and half getting ready for the event. She took her time exfoliating, doing her make-up, and ironing her dress. She was ready to dress to impress, since that's what mattered in the world of education leadership.

She found herself looking in the mirror for a few minutes studying the curves of her hips in her dress. It was a Salmon-colored fitted dress that came right below her knees, with ruffled sleeves. She dressed it with a pair of blue stilettos and mini bag. The perfect combination of class and sass.

She was ready to go.

Trina grabbed her items and made her way to the door. It didn't take long for her to make it to the elevator and the lobby. As soon as she was getting off the elevator, the elevator next to her opened as well. She made a quick glimpse to the side, seeing Damon getting off the elevator into view.

Well I'll be damned, Trina thought to herself as she walked in an attempt to not be seen. Unfortunately, her stilettos mixed with her fitted dress, disabled her ability to walk so fast.

"Trina!" she heard Damon call out from behind her. "I know that's you. I'll know your walk forever girl," he finished as he sped up to catch her.

"Oh hey Damon," Trina said. Even a deaf person could tell she was being fake.

"So you do stay in this hotel too. How ironic is that?" He said while licking his lips and looking Trina up and down. "Maybe we can have a sleepover tonight," he laughed.

"Now you know we have an early morning tomorrow," she responded.

"I'll make sure we both sleep well. I promise," He said with a smile, showing all his perfectly aligned teeth.

Trina laughed it off, looked both ways at the street and proceeded to cross.

"Can I sit next to you at the ceremony?" Damon asked.

"It doesn't matter to me. I'm here for the information and connections," Trina shot back.

"Direct and to the point. Damn! That's why I like you!" He exclaimed.

Trina looked at him sideways and gave a slight grin. "Boy you are something else," she said.

"I think you meant man. That wasn't no little boy I introduced you to," He shot back immediately. "Put some respect on a King," he finished with extra bass in his voice before letting out a laugh.

Trina laughed, "You know what I meant za... Damon." She caught herself. The more he talked, the more turned on she was getting. She didn't know how long she would be able to hold out from her throbbing clit.

"I smell it," he leaned in and whispered to Trina.

She looked at him confused.

"Your juices."

Trina felt herself getting red in the face. They were approaching the conference area, she was horny as hell, and was having a hard time focusing.

As they made their way to the ballroom entrance, they were greeted by conference volunteers.

"Welcome to the opening ceremony!" One of the volunteers exclaimed with a big smile on her face. "It is free seating, so you can go wherever your heart desires! Here is a program for the night," she continued as she handed the program to Trina. She quickly continued talking, "What kind of meal would you like? We have vegetarian, seafood, or chicken."

"I'll take the seafood option," Trina responded.

The volunteer handed Trina a food card. "When it's time for dinner to be served, just give this card to the waiter and they will take care of yuh!" She said happily. "If you have any questions, feel free to ask anyone you see with a purple badge like this," she pointed to her badge on her chest.

"Thank you ma'am," Trina said, ready to find her seat.

"Enjoy yourself ma'am and thank you for coming!" She concluded with a nod.

Trina nodded back to her and made her way inside the ballroom. It was decorated beautifully. The lighting was tinted blue and purple with floral arrangements on each table. The arrangements were rainbow colored and appeared to contain various springtime flowers. With the dim lights, there was lighting pointed to the ceiling that looked like the night sky. It felt like an evening affair outside. The tables were decorated with faux vines, covered with notepads, pens, water, tea, and coffee at the center of the table.

Oh, this is beautiful, she thought to herself as she walked into the sea of tables. There was a table directly in the middle of the room that looked like the perfect view, so she made her way there.

"Is anyone sitting here?" She asked, while pointing to the empty seats at the table.

"Yup, It looks like you are!" Said an older white man sitting a few seats over.

Trina laughed and took a seat.

"Your dress is beeeeautiful!" Exclaimed the woman sitting next to the older white man. "You surely know how to dress!" She said as she scanned the rest of Trina's outfit with a grin on her face.

"Thank you," Trina nodded.

As she turned to get comfortable in her seat, she spotted Damon walking her way.

I am going to have a hard time getting rid of him, I see- she thought to herself as he got closer.

"Oh hey Dean Carlton!" Damon said to another gentleman at the table. "When did you get in?"

"My boy Dame!" Dean Carlton exclaimed as he got up to give Damon a hug. "We got in just a few hours ago, so you know how I'm feeling," he laughed.

"Ha! I can only imagine," Damon said as he took the empty seat next to Trina. "You ready for this session tomorrow?"

"Yea, as ready as I'm going to be man! It's my love for the work that helps me through," Dean Carlton laughed.

Trina instantly recognized that Dean Carlton is the same person as Dr. Calton. He was one of the presenters she was supposed to connect with.

How ironic, she thought to herself as they finished having their conversation.

"Awe man, you know you're the GOAT! You can do this work in your sleep!" Damon responded while slapping Dean Carlton on his back.

"Ha! I'm learning from you, my man!" He responded.

Damon turned to Trina as if he hadn't noticed her at the table until that moment. "Hello Ms. Trina, how are you doing?" He asked, like they didn't just walk into the building together.

"I'm doing fine Mr. Sylvestian. It's nice to see you again," She responded with a smile.

Damon turned to the rest of the table, "There's 6 of us here and I only know 2 other people. Which means, we need some introductions don't you think?"

"Just like Dame, he never meets a stranger twice," Dean Carlton said.

"This is my colleague, Dr. James. He's over our Cultural Competency & Engagement committee and co-presenter for our session tomorrow," Dean Carlton introduced.

"It's a pleasure to meet you," Dr. James said while reaching out for a handshake. "And yourself?" He asked Damon.

"I'm Dr. Damon Sylvestian. I'm the assistant Superintendent of the Depoint School District in Metro Detroit."

"Ok, Ok! We need to find a way to work together. We have been working on our acquisition outreach and how we can do better with our minority student enrollment," Dr. James responded.

"Oh for sure! We are currently hiring an outreach coordinator for the district to be over connecting with universities across the country," Damon responded.

"Talk about perfect timing!" Dean Carlton added.

"This may be the perfect time for me to insert myself into the conversation," said the woman sitting to the right of Dr. James. "I'm Dr. Tabitha from the University of Washington," she said as she reached out her hand to shake everyone's. "This is my husband and rival, Dr. Christian. He's over at Washington State, so you can only imagine our household," she laughed.

"I'm starting to think she only married me for charity reasons," Dr. Christian laughed. "Nice to meet you all. I'm actually planning to attend your session on social media Dr. Sylvestian!"

"Oh don't worry about the Doctor, you can call me Damon," he responded. "I hope you get what you need out of the session."

"I'm sure I will!"

"Hello everyone, I'm Trina Stansby. I'm the outreach manager for Altech, a distributor for major published educational material and curriculum.

"Oh, it looks like you found your outreach coordinator, Dame!" Dean Carlton said in excitement.

"I can't say I wasn't thinking the same," Damon said while looking Trina up and down. "I wonder if we can offer a package that would be hard to refuse," he finished.

Trina felt every ounce of realism and sarcasm in his response.

"We can talk about it," She responded.

The opening ceremony lasted a couple of hours. The president of the AOE spent the time thanking sponsors, attendees, and discussing the importance of collaboration in the educational world. The keynote speaker was the President of Kentucky State University, who discussed measures the country was taking to reduce educational inequality and balancing resources. The typical education talk. Everything that Trina wasn't trying to listen to.

As soon as the ceremony was over, Trina grabbed her things, wished everyone a good night, and headed towards the exit. She was expecting Damon to follow behind her, but to her surprise, he didn't. He was nowhere to be seen and she couldn't help but feel some type of way about it.

How dare this man not leave with me, she thought to herself as she made her way through the exit and across the street. As soon as she made it to the room, she checked her phone to see if he texted her. There was nothing.

"Oh, he is playing now!" Trina said out loud. "I know he knows I want some dick!"

She opened her contact list and called Kisha.

"Hey girl!" Kisha answered the phone.

"Hey girl! What you up to?" She asked.

"Oh you know, the same ole same ole mama thang. Just tryna keep from going crazy" Kisha laughed while picking up clothes and toys from her living room floor.

"You get all my respect hunty," Trina said, in an attempt to calm her bestie's nerves.

"Fuck that respect shit, what's tea?!" Kisha asked.

"Long story short, we ended up sitting next to each other at the opening ceremony and now I'm horny," Trina responded.

"What time are you supposed to be at his place?" Kisha asked?

"Girl, he ain't called, texted, nothing!" Trina shot back.

"You ain't call or text him?" Kisha asked.

"Uh no, what I look like?" Trina asked as she took off her heels and flung them across the room.

"If I was a betting woman, I'd say someone who wanted some conference dick," Kisha responded before laughing.

"Girl, I want dick, but I'm not chasing it. I'm a lady," Trina said before they both burst out laughing together.

"You acting like you tryna make him your man. You just tryna slut him out and go back home," Kisha responded.

Trina got quiet.

"Uh, that is the plan ain't it?" Kisha asked.

"Yea, I think so. I don't know yet," Trina responded.

"Oh you like him like him!" Kisha said while sitting on the arm of her couch.

"I wouldn't say all that, he just got divorced. I ain't forgot about that yet," she responded. "Plus, he brought up a job today. It sounded like he'd give it to me if I said I wanted it," she finished.

"Well look at God! Cause you hate the one you got now!" Kisha shouted.

"That would mean moving to cold ass Michigan! I don't know how I feel about that. San Fran is home and the weather is perfect!" Trina said.

"I mean, but if you have the chance to move somewhere where you can make more money and have consistent dick, I'd say it's worth considering," Kisha joked. "Plus, it'll give me somewhere to vacation away from this house."

"I feel like you keep trying to marry me off, ma'am!" Trina responded.

"I mean, First off! I just want you to know that I support you and whatever deals with your upgrade. Periodt!" Kisha raised her voice.

Trina got quiet for a moment.

"I know girl... and that's why I love you."

"Now gone and hit that man up and tell me about it tomorrow, k?" Kisha implied.

Trina laughed, "Girl, I'll talk to yo crazy self later."

"Alright boo!"

They both ended the call.

Trina stood up and proceeded to take off her dress. As much as she wanted to take Kisha's advice and contact Damon, she couldn't bring herself to do it. She wanted him to chase her.

It didn't take long for Trina to shower and get cuddled in her bed. She found herself checking her phone every 60 seconds, only to find no new notifications. She was becoming irritated, restless, and hornier.

Chapter 6: Tf! Of course I do

The sun arose bright and early, serving as an alarm clock. This was a blessing because Trina was checking her phone so much the night before that she forgot to put it on the charger. If it wasn't for the alarm clock next to her bed, she would have no idea if she overslept or not. Which she didn't.

She had fallen asleep waiting for Damon to contact her, which he never did. She rolled over, plugged her phone up to the charger and laid there looking at the ceiling.

"God, thank you for waking me up today and giving me the energy to face another day!" She exclaimed while rolling out of the bed.

She walked over to the window and watched the cars traveling over the bridge with the sunrise. It was 6:30am and the people were out and about. Her first session started at 9:30, so she had a few hours to get her life together. Damon's session was the first one, then the other two were for strictly connections.

Trina spent the next couple of hours journaling, reading, and getting dressed for the day. She decided to wear a royal blue A-line dress and dressed it up with black and blue mary jane pumps and a black purse. The conference had complimentary continental breakfast, so she decided to grab a meal from the restaurant in her hotel.

It didn't take long for her to get an omelet, eat, and make it to her first session by 9:15. As she arrived, Damon and his co-presenter were still setting up for the presentation. Damon spotted Trina as soon as she walked in the room.

As she signed into the session, Damon made his way over to her.

"Goodmorning beautiful!" He said in his morning sexy tone.

"Good morning Sir," Trina responded as she turned to find an empty seat.

Damon didn't chase her, he just looked sideways and made his way back to the front of the room.

"Thank you to everyone who is here already, we are still setting up for the presentation. Feel free to grab a copy of the presentation at the sign-in table if you haven't yet," his co-presenter announced.

Trina went back to the table and grabbed a printout. By the time 9:30 came around, they were ready and the presentation was on the way. The whole time they were presenting, Trina found herself noticing how fine his partner was. *I'd be wrong if I fucked his friend*, she thought to herself and gave off a chuckle.

"Yea, I would say it's funny too!" Damon said in front of everyone, snapping her back into reality. She had no idea what they were talking about. She just nodded and smiled, hoping he'd move on to the next topic. Which he did.

The presentation lasted until 11am, which was lunch for the next hour. As people were swarming Damon and his partner with questions, she eased out the door and made her way to the restaurant at her hotel. Not even 15 minutes after she was seated, she spotted Damon walking in the door. He bypassed the front hostess, spotted her, and came directly to her table.

"Is this seat taken?" He asked as he pulled it out to take a seat.

"Would it make a difference if I said yes?" Trina asked sarcastically. "You have your nerve diving in here like this. You could be messing up my game," she finished.

"Well excuse me," He said while looking around. "If I'm interrupting anything, I can leave and send you dick pics from the room to make you reconsider," he laughed.

"Boy you are too much!" Trina laughed.

"Man!" He quickly corrected her.

Trina reached her hand under the table, "I'm sorry King." She was now rubbing his thigh, sending chills up his body. After a few strokes she pulled back.

"What happened to you yesterday? Why didn't I hear from you?" She asked.

"I didn't think you wanted to hear from me," he responded. "After you eluded me, I took it that it was too much."

"Or maybe I wanted you to at least reach out and see what was wrong," Trina said faintly.

"Yahl know you be confusing a brother!" He yelled out.

"Yahl? I knew you had someone else" Trina responded.

"Who am I with right now? Who am I in front of right now?" Damon asked.

"Anyways, it was all fun while it lasted," Trina sighed.

Raising his voice, "I'm not letting you get away from me that easy Ms. Thang!"

"Boy Boo. Are you going to order anything or are you just going to look at me?" Trina attempted to change the subject. "We need to grab the waiter if so."

"Thank you, but I'm not hungry. I just needed to find you. I would prefer to be eating you, if we are honest." He said while licking his lips. "Can you take your food to go?" He asked.

Trina thought about it for a moment, looked at her watch. She had 35 minutes until the next session and she had to be there. It was going to take another 5-10 minutes for her food to come out.

"It depends on how quick you can be," she answered.

"Excuse me ma'am," Damon stopped the waitress. "Can you make her order to go and bring the bill please?"

The waitress nodded her head and made her way to the courtesy stand. A few minutes later she had the bill and food in her hand. Damon took the bill, gave her $30 in cash and got up from the table. He came over to Trina and pulled her chair out.

Trina obliged with no hesitation and followed Damon out the restaurant. They got on the elevator and within 10 seconds, his hand was fondling her nipple while the other was under her dress. Trina wasn't wearing panties, which made the access easier as they kissed passionately. Luckily for them, the elevator didn't stop until they made it to his floor.

Damon carried Trina from the elevator into the room and laid her on the bed. He turned her over on her stomach and lifted her dress up. He started kissing her on the back and made his way down to her ass, where he spread her cheeks and stuck his tongue deep into her asshole. He took it out and put it back in while swirling his tongue around in a circle until Trina started moaning.

Trina pulled out her phone to see the time was 11:40. The next session started at noon.

"Baby, we have to hurry up, I need to make the next session for work," Trina said.

"Fuck that job. I'm giving you a new one," he said while he started licking up her back to her neck. "But I'll respect your time and make it fast," he finished while flipping her over on her back.

"If we are honest, I really only want head right now," Trina said while pushing his head down to her vagina.

He obliged by spreading her pussy lips and sticking his whole face in her pussy. He came up for air and started sucking on her clit like a vacuum cleaner. Trina squirmed as her leg started getting weak. While sucking her clit, he took his finger and put it in her mouth before sticking it inside her vagina.

It was something about the way he sucked on her oversized clit and hit her g-spot that made the passion uncontrollable. Her body started to stiffen and she felt her cum flowing down to the point she couldn't hold it. She wrapped her legs around his neck and he started sucking in a more serious vibrational flow. With her legs wrapped around his neck he took his arm and tucked it under her, pulling her closer to him.

"Ooooh King, you know exactly how I like it!" Trina yelled out. "I'm about to cum baby!"

"Cum for daddy, baby. Cum all in my mouth!" He responded while still humming on her pussy.

He moved his pinky and stuck it in her butt while his thumb stimulated her vagina. He started penetrating her holes faster and faster until she couldn't take it anymore.

"Ahhhh! I'm cumming baby!" She screamed out while trying to get away from him. He wasn't letting her go anywhere, He grabbed her body, pulled her to the edge of the bed and picked her up into the air.

"Wrap your legs around me tighter!" He demanded as he stood up straight, sucking on her pussy.

Trina couldn't take it much longer so she bent down and grabbed his head as a way to brace herself.

"I want you to cum again all over my face baby. Then we can go." He said.

"We don't have enough time!" She moaned.

Little did she know, he had it all perfectly timed out like he knew her body better than she knew it herself.

"Daddy knows what he is doing," he confidently responded.

He took his finger and put it back in her ass. While he pressed on her g-spot he started singing a tune on her clit and one minute later, she was squirting all over his face.

"Ahhhhh, put me down please baby!" She pleaded with Damon.

He listened and sat her down on the bed. He spread her legs open and licked every bit of cum that was oozing out of her pussy until it was no more.

"Do you feel better?" He asked after kissing her passionately.

"Yes, but now I don't know if I can walk," she responded.

"We have a couple of minutes before we have to make it to the next session." He said while heading to the bathroom.

While spread across the bed, Trina asked, "What do you be doing to me?!"

Damon turned on the bathroom sink and peaked out the doorway. "Giving you want you have been really wanting," he said before disappearing back into the bathroom.

"Whew chile, you ain't neva lied," Trina said under her breathe.

Damon was lathering up a face cloth to wash his face and Trina just watched him through the mirror in the bathroom.

"So babe, there's this party I want you to attend with me tomorrow night, if you're down to try something different." Damon said while peeking out the doorway and washing his face.

"Sure, what kind of party? What is the vibe and dress code?" She asked.

"Uh, put on something sexy and Just promise me that you'll be open-minded. I want to introduce you to parts of my world." Damon said.

"What does that mean? What be going on in your world?" Trina asked while sitting up in bed.

"I just feel like you match my vibe and you just may like it," He responded.

"You're still not answering my question!" Trina shot back. "Where are you trying to take me?" She asked while getting off the bed.

"And what was that about you giving me a new job? Or was that just sex talk?" Trina continued talking.

"Well, if you give me a chance to answer one question at a time, I could do that for you," he sarcastically responded.

Trina looked at him with a straight faced expression.

"Boy, don't play with me."

"You are going to get enough of calling a King, boy," He shot back.

Trina didn't say a word.

"I want to introduce you to another world. A world that I feel you could come to enjoy with me. I used to do this twice a year before my divorce and want you to experience it with me, as long as you can keep it a secret."

"The fuck is that supposed to mean?" Trina asked while going into the bathroom and onto the toilet.

Damon rang the water out of the towel, turned the water off, and hung the towel up before exiting the bathroom. "I guess we will see when tomorrow comes."

Trina's brain started spinning and she found herself with so many questions about what he was asking of her. Where was he trying to take her and why was it such a secret?

She finished using the bathroom, washed her hands and made her way back to her phone. It was exactly noon and she was officially late for the first afternoon session.

"See, I knew this was a bad idea!" She yelled at Damon while scrambling to get her items. I'm late and I don't feel like hearing my boss's mouth!"

" I already told you, I want you to come to Michigan and work with me. I think we would make a good team." Damon responded in a lowered tone.

"We will cross that bridge when it gets here," she responded as she made her way to the door. "I have to go. I'll text you later."

"Alright baby, we'll talk more about it later."

Trina disappeared through the door and rushed towards the elevator. She was walking so fast that it looked like she was running. She made it to the session at 12:12, just as they were finishing introductions. The room was full, but she was able to find a seat in the back left corner along the wall.

The presentation went well and Trina was able to make conversation with the presenters as expected. They were able to schedule a phone meeting for the next week to discuss a potential partnership. It was the same thing for the last session as well. It seemed as if everything went along perfectly for her.

When she finished the last session at 3:15 she went to the closing ceremony for the day and made it back to her hotel room by 6pm. She was beyond tired and all she could think about was sleep and what Damon was inviting her to the next day.

She pulled out her phone and sent Damon a text. "Hey King, how was the rest of your day?" She texted as she made her way to run a bath. It didn't take long for him to respond back. It was like he had their text thread open already.

"It was good, beautiful, how about yours?" He asked.

"It was really productive. Made some good connections for work!" She responded with one of her hands under the running water. It wasn't until the jacuzzi tub was full when he responded back.

"You should really consider coming to work with our district..." he responded.

Trina read the message and threw the phone on the bed as she undressed to get in the tub. Once she finished undressing she grabbed her phone to text him back. To her surprise, he had texted her again. "I can make sure you get a good package."

Trina responded back before getting in the tub. "We can talk about it before I fly out on Sunday. Btw, what time do I need to be ready tomorrow?"

"You promise? Lol" He responded immediately. "7pm is perfect!"

"Alright sounds good. I'll see you tomorrow at 7pm" Trina responded before throwing her phone on the bed and stepping into the tub.

"Wooooo..." She let out as she stepped into the water. It was nice and hot, just to her liking. As she stretched out in the jacuzzi, she turned on the jet streams and was in heaven. She had to have been in the tub for at least an hour when she finally decided to get out after seeing her shriveled skin.

She dried her body off and lathered herself up with her homemade body butter that made her skin feel like silk. She laid across the bed and sensually rubbed her body from her feet to the back of her neck.

Life is really good, she thought to herself as she watched the sunset through the large windows. She didn't even look at her phone again, until she found herself waking up at 2am. She was so relaxed that she fell asleep unknowingly. Shortly after her last message to Damon, he asked if he could see her to finish what they started earlier. That was hours ago and she didn't have the energy to do anything but go back to sleep.

Chapter 7: Oh, this what you on??

Trina was so busy with sessions and making key connections that the day went by faster than she thought. She hadn't talked to Damon all day. He hadn't reached out to her and she hadn't reached out to him. It was 5pm when she was walking into her hotel room from the day. He didn't seem like the type to flake, so she was confident that he wasn't going to stand her up for their date.

She went straight to the bathroom and started taking off her clothes, turned on the shower and got in. The water was nice and hot and the water hit her body perfectly with the waterfall shower head. It took her a little over an hour to get ready, as it was hard for her to decide on which after hours dress to wear. She only brought two dresses, one was a short little black dress and the other was a blue sun dress.

He did say dress sexy, she thought to herself as she remembered their conversation. She decided to go with the little black dress with a pair of black Alexander McQueen pumps. By the time she put her shoes on it was 6:30 giving herself time to pre-game before they met up. Trina made her way down to the hotel bar and had a couple drinks as she waited for 7pm to hit.

At 7pm on the dot, Damon texted Trina, "Meet me downstairs at the bar." She responded back, "I'm already here, see you shortly."

It took him only a couple of minutes to walk into the bar. As soon as he made his way to her he looked her up and down, licked his lips and gave her the tightest hug she had ever received from a man.

"Girl, I could just eat you up right here, right now!" He exclaimed.

Trina blushed and hit him on his shoulders while giggling. "Boy, come on, let's get going."

"You're not going to get your bill?" He asked.

"Oh, it's going on my room tab, don't worry about it." Trina responded.

He went into his wallet, pulled out a $50 bill and placed it in her bozzum. "I can't have my woman buying her own drinks," he said as he grabbed her hand to guide her outside the bar and to the front door.

"Our driver should be pulling up any moment," he said as he scanned the street.

Not long after, a silver Cadillac Escalade pulled up with tinted windows. The driver got out and came to the back of the car to open the door. "Good evening Mr. Sylvestian and Miss."

"Good afternoon Mr. Jacobson. I hope you are doing well today," Damon responded as they got into the back of the truck.

The truck was absolutely beautiful. It was stocked with a fruit basket, champagne, a tv, and a partition between them and the front.

"Do you remember where I said we were going?" Damon asked.

"Yes Sir! It's going to take about 40 minutes to arrive, so just sit back and enjoy the complimentary champagne and TV," Mr. Jacobson responded.

Damon simply responded, "Sounds good," while rolling up the partition.

He turned and looked at Trina.

"Why are you looking so serious?" She asked as she reached for a grape vine from the basket.

"It's probably best for me to let you know where we are going. It's not fair of me to just pop it up on you." He started.

Trina looked at him sideways as if he could hear her asking, *what is it?* In her head.

"So, we are going to an exclusive club where everyone is only there if they are invited. It can get a little wild, I have to let you know that." He continued.

"Okkkk, is it something I should be afraid of?" She asked with an eyebrow raised.

"No no, it's nothing like that. But, I must let you know that everything you see has to stay there. It's some high profile people who will be there and privacy is top-most priority," he continued.

"You talking like we are going to some type of sex drug club or something," she laughed.

Damon bit the bottom of his lip and looked Trina directly in her eyes.

"We're going to a sex club? That's where you're taking me?" She asked, slightly upset. "What do I look like?"

"Someone who is into the same things that I am into. The same things that a lot of people in this field of work are interested in," he quickly responded.

Trina had never been to a sex club and found herself intrigued by the idea of attending one, even though she felt a way towards Damon.

"We don't have to do anything," he assured Trina with a kiss on the cheek. "But, I really feel like you're going to like it," he said confidently.

"And if I don't, this will be the last day you ever talk to me!" Trina raised her voice and turned to face the window.

"Baby, after the love we have made, I'm 100% sure you are going to enjoy the experience. If you want, I'll even let you punish me." He said with a smirk on his face.

Damon could tell she was upset, as he expected, so he did everything he could to try and get her attention again. Damon offered to rub her feet; she declined. He tried to get closer to her; she moved away. After a few attempts, he got the clue and stopped trying. Trina didn't say anything for the rest of the ride.

They made it to their destination around 8pm. The sun had set and the sky was a beautifully glazed purple and blue. The building looked like an older warehouse with steel posts outside the building. It was dimly lit and it was hard to distinguish the entrance in the lighting.

The driver came around to open the door for them. "What time should I be back to get you all?" He asked.

"11pm is good," Damon responded as he helped Trina out of the car. She attempted to get out without his help, but the step down was too high for her in her heels. As she stepped down she snatched her hand from Damon's and stood waiting for him to lead the way. At this point, she felt there was nothing she could do but see what it was all about.

The driver got back into the car and prepared to drive off as Damon started walking to the front door. The door looked camouflaged with the outer walls of the building. Damon did some type of secret knock at the door and someone opened it from the other side. The front entrance area looked highly luxurious and plush. The floors, walls, and benches were all red velvet with purple lighting placed sporadically. It was dimly lit and the music could be heard from the back.

Damon made way to the front desk to check-in. "Hello Sir, how are you doing tonight?" The staff person asked Damon as he approached the desk.

"I'm doing great, can't complain." Damon responded.

"That's great to hear. My name is Kendrick, the guard host for the evening's affair," Kendrick responded. "Can I have your ID please?"

Damon presented his ID and Kendrick cross checked it from his guest list. As he skimmed the names on the list, Damon turned around and kissed Trina on the cheek.

"This is my guest, Ms. Trina Stansby," he said as he pointed to Trina.

"Ok, she's going to have to sign a new confidentiality agreement in order to participate in the club tonight. Before going in, I'm also going to need to collect your phones as well. You can get them back at the end of the night."

Trina reached for her ID and passed it to Kendrick. He handed her a 10-page contract and took her ID to make a copy of it. Trina went over to the bench and read over the contract.

"Babe, you really don't need to read over it. All it says is that everything you see here stays here. No electronics are allowed, no watching patrons in the act if their curtain is closed... You know all of that stuff," Damon said in an attempt to rush Trina through the process.

"And I'm still going to read it," She said as she continued reading through each bullet point.

- *Only women are allowed upstairs alone.*
- *Men must be accompanied by a woman in the dom room.*
- *The safe word for the club is "stop now!" use this safe word when you want your partner to stop.*
- *All doms are required to get a verbal agreement of limitations from subs before role play*

- *Everyone is required to communicate with their alias name. No real names are used inside the club.*

- *What happens here, stays here.*

- *Women approach first, in this club. Men must not make a move until the woman has vocalized her interest.*

- *You are allowed to use all prompts in the club; make sure to sanitize everything you use when you are done.*

The list continued on and on and Trina found herself skimming through the pages. After the 2nd page, she got tired of reading and decided to take Damon's word for it. She got her ID back from Kendrick and signed the last page of the contract and handed it back to him.

"Mr. Sylvestian, your total for this evening is $350 for Ms. Trina. Your membership fees cover today's experience," Kendrick said.

Trina was amazed at how much it cost to attend the club. $350 sounded like a lot, but Damon reached for his wallet with no problem.

He handed his card over to Kendrick and once the payment was processed, he handed him his card back.

"Ok Mr. and Miss, Your alias names for the evening are Todd and Virginia. Make sure to use these names when anyone asks you for your identification. It's for your continued protection," Kendrick assured them both.

Once they finished signing in, the guard led them down a dark hallway into another room. This room was decorated with antique chairs and tables that looked as if they were from the early 1900's. They were in amazing condition and set the mood beautifully.

"The bartender will be with you shortly for your drink orders. Once you finish your drink orders you can go into the freedom lounge." The guard said.

Not even a minute later, the bartender appeared to take their orders. The bartender was a slim thick mixed girl with curly hair. She had on all black leather, with a dog collar covered in spikes and glitter. Her dress was bone tight and came midway down her thighs.

"Hello beautiful people! My name is Anna and I will be your personal bartender and guide for the night. Can I start you off with your first drink?" Anna asked.

"I'll take a Tequila Sunrise," Trina said. Damon ordered a double cognac.

Anna disappeared to the bar to get their drinks and returned rather quickly.

"I'm going to let you both enjoy your drink and I'll be back in 10 minutes to guide you into the lounge area," Anna said.

Just as Anna disappeared between the veil, Trina noticed a familiar face walking through the door.

Now this is going to be interesting, Trina thought to herself as she tossed back her drink.

Chapter 8: Oh, this wild!

There was Mr. Crenshee, the president of The University of Missouri, walking into the sex club. She just had lunch with him earlier that day to discuss partnership opportunities for work and now she was being introduced to another side of him. When he noticed her and Damon sitting in the lounge, he approached them with a smile.

"Hey there good people, I'm Tim, what's your names?" Mr. Crenshee asked them.

Trina knew his real name wasn't Tim, which reminded her of her alias for the night.

"I'm Todd and this is Virginia," Damon said, while shaking Tim's hand.

"Are you both participating in the festivities tonight? Or just here to enjoy the ambiance?" Tim asked.

"You know me, I'm here for the vibes and whatever comes from that," Damon laughed.

Trina was confused at what they were talking about so she just stood back and smiled. The woman that was with Mr. Crenshee was quiet and aloof. *I wonder if she was surprised into coming here too*, Trina thought to herself as she observed her.

"Ooh, where are my manners?" Mr. Crenshee asked. "This is Kalia, my beautiful partner for the night," he finished as he presented Kalia to Trina and Damon.

Just as he finished, Anna and another server appeared from the back room. The other server went to tend to Mr. Crenshee and Anna made her way to Damon and Trina.

"How are you both feeling?" She asked the pair.

"I'm doing quite well, thank you." Trina replied. Damon simply gave a head nod and made an invisible toast with his glass in the air.

"Well if you're ready, I can escort you into the lounge," Anna continued.

Both Trina and Damon stood up to follow behind her. They walked down another dark hallway that was dimly lit and decorated with antique wall fixtures and intimate paintings. As they entered the lounge, Trina couldn't believe what she was experiencing.

There was a cage to her right and left, that had women inside dancing nude in a seductive manner. As they walked further, she noticed tables and benches lined around the room where people were sitting. There were 4 doors on each wall of the room that looked identical to each other, but had numbers and names on them. As they got past the cages, Trina noticed a woman walking with two men connected with dog collars and chains. She was dressed in all black and had a whip in her hand, which she used on them every few steps they took.

Anna stopped and turned around to face both Trina and Damon. "Have you both been here before? Or would you like a tour of the space?"

"Yes, I've been here before, but she hasn't. We don't really need a tour," Damon responded.

A part of Trina didn't like how he made the decision for her that she didn't need a tour, but she also liked the fact that he could show her around.

Trina looked around the room to see there were quite a few people from their conference present at the club.

"Is everyone in education a freak?" She asked Damon. He just looked at her, shook his head, and laughed.

"Will you be using any of our prompts tonight?" Anna asked. "We have our bondage accessories over in this room," she continued as she pointed to the room with the number 5 on it. "Our sex lounge can be found upstairs, in which you may find yourself enjoying quite a bit," she finished.

"Thank you so much Anna! Could you get us another drink? We are going to take a seat over here for a moment as we take in the ambiance." Damon said.

"Sure thing Sir," she responded and disappeared towards the bar.

Damon and Trina found an empty table along the side of the room, in front of one of the doors. The music was loud, but Trina could hear something behind the door they were near. It was the sound of whips and moans.

"What's going on back there?" She asked Damon.

"Oh, those are private room sessions. Someone is most likely being punished. That type of stuff turns some people on," he responded while finishing off his drink.

As they were talking, Trina noticed a woman staring at her from the other side of the room. She was at a table with two gentlemen, but she couldn't keep her eyes off them and she wasn't ashamed. The men she was with were dressed similarly to each other in all black. She was wearing red and black with bright red lipstick on.

Trina turned her attention back to Damon, who was mesmerized by the women dancing in the cages.

She tapped him on the shoulder to get his attention. "Damon, that woman over there is staring at us," Trina said while discretely pointing across the room. Damon squinted his eyes slightly and started smiling. "Oh, that's Dean Stringfew! She a dom and those are her two subs for the night it looks like," he responded before turning back to the cage dancers.

Trina could tell she was going to have a hard time keeping his attention from the dancers, so she decided to roam. She didn't even let Damon know, she just got up and started walking. She walked across the main floor to the other side of the room where a few of the doors were open. She was able to get a peek into one of the rooms. The room was very posh and was decorated in a forest green and black with fur carpet. Inside was a bed with chains dangling from all of the corners. On the wall were hooks with different gadgets stringing from them. She noticed a whip, handcuffs, and a restraint jacket, the other items were foreign to her.

She turned and kept walking to see that all the rooms looked quite similar to the first. She made her way to the stairs and walked up to see what she would find. Upstairs was a different vibe from downstairs. There were people walking around freely naked. They were all smiling at Trina as she walked past them. The men had no problem allowing their limp dicks to be seen. There were dozens of rooms with curtains instead of a door.

Trina walked down the hallways lined with rooms and came to the first room with an open curtain and saw something she wasn't expecting. There was a couple having full blown sex in the room for everyone to see. The woman was sitting on the bed and the man was giving her oral sex. Then, out of nowhere, another man appeared and stood over the woman with his penis in her face. She took it and started sucking it passionately. All you could hear were the moans and sounds of satisfaction.

For some reason this was turning Trina on and she decided to keep exploring. The next open room she walked up to was a room with two men. They were both kissing passionately in the bed, while touching and rubbing on each other with all of their clothes on. Trina kept walking.

The next room she came across was with 2 women. One of the women had a strap-on on and was penetrating the other woman from the back. She was penetrating her with intense strength and little to no intimacy. Trina felt her coochie getting sore as she saw her penetrate in and out.

"Say my name bitch!" She heard the woman scream out to the other. This was a little too much for Trina so she decided to keep walking.

The next room gave Trina an interesting feeling. It was a woman and a man kissing passionately. They were still dressed, but it was something sexy about their chemistry that turned Trina on. They both were standing up and the man started taking the woman's clothes off and touching every inch of her body that the clothing touched.

Trina felt herself getting wet as she watched them seduce and fall into intimacy with each other. Next thing she knew, they were both undressed and she felt herself fantasizing as if she was enjoying the experience with them. Trina started touching on herself and biting her lip as the couple went further. All of a sudden, the woman in the room motioned for Trina to come inside. Trina looked around her to see if there was anyone else she could be motioning to, but it wasn't. It was only Trina standing there watching them.

Trina had never participated in public sex before, let alone with strangers. As convincing as she was, Trina wasn't convinced just yet. As she took a step back, she stumbled a little over someone who was walking behind her. She turned around and to her surprise, it was the woman from downstairs who was staring at her, Dean Stringfew!

"Are you enjoying yourself so far?" She asked in a soft tone, looking Trina up and down.

"It's definitely a new experience for me," Trina said with her head tilted down.

The woman grabbed Trina's chin and lifted her head while saying, "There's a first time for everything." She blew her a kiss and kept walking down the hallway.

Trina had never been with a woman and for the first time ever, the energy of another woman turned her on. Heated and horny from the exchange, Trina went back downstairs to be with Damon. He was sitting at a table conversing with Mr. Crenshee and another gentleman. She took a seat next to him and motioned for the waitress to order a drink.

"Welcome back, My Love, are you enjoying yourself?" Damon asked with a smirk on his face.

Trina let out a laugh, "It's been very interesting to say the least!"

Damon turned to his colleagues, "Excuse me gentleman, I'm going to tend to my lady for a moment, I'll be back shortly." He stood up and motioned for Trina to follow him to the next table.

They took a seat and he started staring her in the eyes. "What's making it interesting? Did anything happen?" He asked.

"I've just never seen anyone have public sex like this before. Upstairs is crazy!" She said with excitement in her voice.

"You want to go back up there?" Damon asked while licking his lips.

"And do what?" Trina tried to ask innocently, even though she knew exactly what he was talking about.

"We could see what it feels like to have someone else watch us," He responded bluntly.

Trina never thought she would be considering something such as this, in a million years. How did she go from not having sex in forever to fucking in a sex club? As she was looking up from her deep thoughts, Anna was arriving with her drink. Without hesitation, Trina threw back her drink and it was gone in less than a minute. Damon just sat there looking at her as she tossed it back.

Trina slammed her glass on the table and stood up. She grabbed his hand and walked him towards the steps leading upstairs. The energy upstairs was just as what it was when she left. It just felt like sex and ecstasy. They walked the long hallway and found the room in the back corner empty. A part of Trina wanted to close the curtains, but another part of her wanted everyone to see them make love. She wanted them to see the fire and magic they made when they were together.

Damon didn't waste time getting to it when they walked in the room. He took off his jacket and proceeded to kiss Trina passionately. It was more sloppy than passionate, a stranger would think he was desperate by the way he was devouring her. He started gripping her breasts and squeezing them tightly, moving his hand to grasp every part of her body. Something about him was really aggressive. It was like he had something to prove.

He pushed Trina onto the bed, pulled up her dressed, took off her panties, and exposed her pussy. He got on his knees and started sucking on her pussy like he hadn't eaten in 2 days. The pleasure felt like it was multiplied for some reason because Trina was having a hard time controlling herself. She put her hand on his head and started directing him as he ate her like a holiday meal.

Trina let out the most fulfilled moaned just as Dean Stringfew walked past. She must've had a slow reaction to what was going on because she doubled back and stood in the doorway watching them. Trina looked up and saw her in the doorway and froze. She was really being watched as she got her pussy eaten.

"Can I come in?" She asked

Damon looked up and smiled. He looked over at Trina for her approval. After a few moments of looking at them both back and forth, she let out a simple, "sure."

The woman came into the room and got on the bed before whispering to Trina, "My name is Marie, it's nice to meet you."

She didn't wait for Trina to finish before she had her breasts in her mouth. She started sucking on her breasts as Damon finished eating her pussy. She was in heaven. The level of pleasure she was feeling made her feel as if she was on cloud 9, literally. She couldn't feel her legs and it felt like she was floating. She was no longer on the bed. Damon came up for air and joined Marie by sucking on her neck. Marie took her fingers and inserted them into Trina's vagina and motioned her fingers like she was playing the clarinet. She was drumming on her g-spot and Trina felt herself cumming.

"You like that Mama?" Marie asked before going down to taste Trina's cum and wetness. "Oooh, I like that!" She exclaimed as she licked the cum off her fingers.

Damon took out his penis, that was already hard and ready for action. Trina without thought, grabbed it and pulled him in front of her and started sucking it. At this point, she was on the edge of the bed, Marie was on her knees, and Damon was standing on the bed thrusting his dick in and out of Trina's mouth. It was like a porn scene she had masturbated to plenty of times before.

After a few minutes, Trina looked at the doorway to see there were a few people watching them. They were becoming the hot menage trois. From the sounds of Damon's moaning to Marie's slurping sounds, it sounded like they were creating music. All of a sudden, Marie stood up and Marie ordered Damon to lay on the bed. She took the restraints on each of the bed corners and fastened them to his wrists and ankles, disabling him from moving.

"Are you ok with what is about to happen?" She asked Him. He nodded in agreement and said yes.

She turned to Trina and asked her, "You want his dick or his face?"

Apparently Trina took too long to answer, so Marie started giving orders. "I want you to ride him until you can't anymore, while I drown him in my cum... is that ok?" She asked Trina, as she pulled a condom from the stand next to the bed. She unwrapped it and pulled it over his dick, before instructing Trina to sit on top of him like it was her first time riding a dick.

"I want you to make his dick yours. Make him beg you to stop, you hear me?" She asked Trina as she undressed in front of them all.

When she finished undressing, she took Trina's hips and guided her down on Damon's Dick. Trina let out a moan of passion as Marie guided her hips back and forth.

She kissed Trina on the neck and said softly, "You have to let him know who really runs everything."

Without thinking, Trina responded, "Yes ma'am."

"There you go Mama!" She said like a proud teacher as she climbed on top of his face and started sucking Trina's breast. "You like to get slutted out, huh?" Marie asked Damon.

"It's your world right now," he mumbled as he moved his face from her vagina.

"That's not what I asked you!" She yelled back as she rode faster on his face. "Speed it up, apparently he doesn't know how to answer questions." Marie demanded.

"Yes ma'am!" Damon yelled out through her thighs.

"That's better," she said. "Now eat my ass like you haven't eaten in days," she finished as she spread her ass cheeks open. "Grip his dick tighter mama, he needs to know who is in charge right now."

Damon let out an uncontrollable moan as Marie started pinching his nipples and rubbing them between her fingers.

"Bounce on that dick!" She instructed Trina. "Faster!"

Trina sped up and felt herself getting ready to cum all over his dick. Something came over her and she was instantly turned up a notch. She got off his dick and instructed Marie to stand up.

"Get on your knees," she said to Marie as she lifted her leg on the chair. "Eat my pussy until I tell you to stop," she instructed her. "I want you to watch her make me cum," she turned and said to Damon.

He obliged and lifted his head as far as he could from the restraints. Trina took off her dress completely as Marie was eating her out and started playing with her nipples.

"You like watching her eat me out?" She asked Damon in a sexy tone.

He nodded his head up and down in quick motions.

"You like seeing me happy?" She asked him.

"From the day I first met you." He answered.

"That didn't answer my question!" She demanded.

"Yes ma'am!" He responded after a couple of seconds, as he caught his breath.

He was too late, because Trina had reached for the whip on the wall before he could get the ma'am out.

Wooshhh went the whip as Trina lashed Damon on his thigh. He flinched.

As she hit Damon, it seemed like it excited Marie because Marie started eating her out faster. Trina took her hand and put it on top of Marie's head and started guiding her through her orgasm.

"Omg! I'm cumming!" Trina screamed as her legs started trembling. Marie took her finger and stuck it up Trina's ass to intensify the orgasm. Trina couldn't take it and felt her legs start to give in.

"Get up!" She yelled at Marie. "I want you to ride him until he cums."

Marie listened without question and got on top of Damon's hard dick with a new condom. Trina got on the bed and started sucking Marie's breasts as she rode Damon's dick nice and slow. With each stroke she let out a moan and Damon was squirming like it was becoming hard for him to hold it in. Trina took her head and started sucking Marie's clit as she rode Damon. She always wanted to know what another woman's pusssy tasted like and it wasn't as bad as she thought it would be. Marie was enjoying it and it forced her to start riding Damon with more intensity until they both couldn't hold it in anymore. By this time, Trina had her ass in Damon's face while she was sucking Marie's clit.

Next thing she knew, they were all cumming at the same time.

Trina unleashed Damon from the bed and all three of them laid in the bed together for the next 20 minutes touching and kissing each other. They had a larger audience by this time as it appeared others were touching on themselves as they watched.

"Looks like our sex tape would sell real good!" Trina laughed out loud.

She looked on the wall to notice that their session had went so long, that it was almost time for their driver to come pick them up shortly. This forced them to get up and get dressed. They were back downstairs within 10 minutes. With a few minutes to spare they struck up a conversation with Dean Stringfew and Mr. Crenshee.

"That was some time you all had up there!" Mr. Crenshee said in excitement. "It made me and my lady go get some quick action when we saw you," he laughed. "Yea, she's a natural," Marie said while touching Trina on her neck.

"I will say, this was my first time and it was nothing like I thought it would be," Trina nervously laughed.

Laughing, Marie turned to Trina, "We are going to have to catch up sometime outside of here. I'd love to keep in contact with you."

Trina wrote her phone number down on a Napkin for Marie.

"I promise it won't be about sex," she laughed. "I know you work for that publishing company and we may be able to do some business together," she finished.

Damon cleared his throat, "Oh that won't be for long." He grabbed Trina's chin and kissed her. "Mr. Jacobson should be outside," he said and then turned to the other two. "I enjoyed our evening tonight. Let's catch dinner tomorrow after the conference closing to discuss business," he said to the two and nodded.

"Sounds good to me!" Mr. Crenshee responded with his drink raised.

"I'll see you both later," Marie said while looking Trina up and down.

The pair made their way outside and there was Jacobson, just as Damon projected, outside waiting for them at the door. The pair made it back to the hotel right before midnight. Trina decided to stay the night with Damon to seal the night.

Chapter 9: I might as well

Trina woke up at 5:45am on the dot as if her alarm was set, but it wasn't. She released herself from Damon's arms and got out of the bed quietly. She tiptoed around the room to gather her things before sneaking out of the room by 6am. She was able to do all of this without waking him up.

Trina got back to her room, turned on her phone and placed it on the charger. The last thing she needed was a dead cellphone for the entire day. Unfortunately, as soon as she placed her phone on the charger it started ringing. She looked down at the phone and of course it was Kisha. She answered immediately.

"Heeeey Pooh! Good morning!" Trina answered the phone.

"Uh huh! Don't hey pooh me, why didn't I hear from you last night!" She asked with an attitude.

"Oop! Not you have an attitude with me about what I decided to do for the night." Trina responded back.

"I mean excuse me for being worried about my bestfriend! All I knew was that you were going to some secret location with that man. I couldn't track your GPS, because someone mysteriously turned it off!" Kisha yelled back. "You broke the most important rule last night," she finished.

"Are you done yet?" Trina asked sarcastically.

"Maybe!" Kisha immediately answered. "Only reason I am done is because I'm ready for the tea on how yesterday went. What did yahl do?" Kisha asked as she opened the fridge and pulled out a gallon of orange juice and a glass from the cabinet.

"So, he definitely took me to a sex club!" Trina said in a high pitched tone.

"A what?!" Kisha yelled! "What you mean a sex club? And why are you just now telling me this?" She asked.

"Well, he didn't tell me until we were enroute and in order to enter the club we had to turn in our phones. I was not thinking hunty!" Trina responded.

"Uh huh," Kisha said in disbelief. "Well, what happened? What was it like?" She asked.

"It was really interesting! We had to sign a contract to enter. It's expensive as fuck and I'm learning that alot of professionals are into some kinky shit," Trina said. "It was one hell of an experience," she finished as she thought about her experience with Marie and Damon.

"So, do people really be having real life sex in there?" Kisha asked.

"Yup! They be ass-naked too! It was two hallways of rooms full of people having sex. Then there's an area where people do more networking than fucking," Trina laughed.

"Whew chile, that sounds like something serious!" Kisha responded. "Well at least you had an opportunity to experience it!" She finished.

"It was definitely a bucket list type of experience," Trina laughed harder.

"That laugh sounds suspicious. What did you do at that club, Trina?!" Kisha demanded.

"Girl nothing, it's just so interesting to have experienced one and to watch people having sex in front of me. It definitely turned me on though," she answered.

"Uh huh, for some reason I feel like more happened but you just don't want to tell me," Kisha said suspiciously while sipping her juice.

Trina got quiet. "So what have you been up to?" She changed the subject.

"Not you changing the subject now!" Kisha shouted. 'Thank you for inadvertently answering my question heffa!"

Trina shot back without hesitation, "Girl boo!"

"I've been good though. We are taking a random family trip to the mountains, so I'm about to start preparing our food and getting ready for the trip," Kisha responded.

"That must be fun to do those types of things as a family," Trina said with a smile on her face.

"Girl whatever. It's just more work for me. I'm ready to get out of this house. That's the best part about it all for me," she laughed.

"How long are yahl going to be gone?" Trina asked.

"Kev took Monday off, so we are going for a couple of nights. We are going to pitch a tent in the reserve and live between there and the camper," she answered.

"Oh that sounds like a really good time in nature!" Trina said excitedly.

"Uh huh, not as good as Ms. Sex Club Experience!" Kisha said sarcastically as she got up and walked back into the Kitchen.

"Anyways, let me know when you all make it safely. I need to charge my phone and start getting ready for the opening session today. I have one more I need to attend for work, then I can breathe!" Trina responded.

"If you're tired of talking to me, just say that!" Kisha shot back.

"Girl, It's what I told you it is. Get out of your feelings," Trina demanded.

"Uh huh. Well, I will talk to you later girl. Stay safe today, even though you're going to do whatever you want to do anyways," Kisha advised.

"Yes Ma'am!" Trina responded. "We will talk as soon as both of us are back home."

"Talk to you later," Kisha said before ending the call. She didn't say any "I love you's" and she didn't wait for Trina to respond back.

Trina already knew that Kisha had an attitude because Trina wasn't telling her all the details about the sex club. Honestly, Trina didn't want to share it with anyone. It was something she wanted to keep to herself as a secret. She still wasn't 100% with how she felt about everything and the last thing she needed was someone else in her business lecturing her about what she is doing that is right and wrong. Her best bet at that moment was to keep it all to herself as she figured it all out.

It didn't take Trina too long to get ready for the day. She did all of her morning grooming routines, beat her face, and dressed like she was going for everyone's job. She decided to wear her emerald green fitted dress with ruffles at the bottom paired with her floral pumps and a floral shawl in case it was cold. The opening ceremony started at 8:15 and it was 7:30 by the time Trina finished grooming. She decided she was going to grab a quick breakfast from the continental breakfast bar before heading across the street for the conference.

Trina made it to the opening ceremony hall around 8am, which gave her ample time to find a really good seat with a great view of the main stage area. As the people started filling into the room, Trina found herself noticing familiar faces from the night before that she hadn't noticed before attending the party. *Oh, we are all some freaks* in real life, she thought to herself while pouring herself hot water for a cup of tea.

Just as she started steeping her tea bag, she noticed Dean Stringfew walking into the hall. She was walking with two other individuals and it looked like they were having a very serious conversation. She didn't look happy at all and Trina knew this wasn't the best time to go up and say anything. As she got closer to Trina's table, she noticed her and gave her a smile and wink and kept walking.

Damon walked into the room 10 minutes later and was able to spot Trina with no problem. It's like he was a hound dog and he memorized her scent. He was wearing a slate gray suit partnered with a tangerine print tie and socks.

That man knows he be dressing his ass off! Trina thought to herself as he made his way towards her.

"Good morning Baby," he greeted Trina while reaching down and kissing her.

Trina froze. Public displays of affection? In front of these people? This was the last thing she was expecting.

"Don't look like that. I see you saved me a seat," He continued as he sat down in the seat next to her. "So, I have some good news for you!" He said excitedly.

"What's that?" Trina asked.

"I told the superintendent that I met someone who I felt would be perfect for the outreach position we have available. I really think you would be perfect."

Trina interrupted him, "How are you making these decisions without me?"

"I just really feel like it's meant to happen! You have the skills for the job. It starts at $100k in a city with a low cost of living. It comes with a $10k moving stipend and complimentary movers to transition you!"

"But, I'm just getting settled at my current job…" Trina started.

"I'll also pay for your 1st year of housing. You can have a beautiful condo on the Detroit River overlooking the sunset over Canada!" He exclaimed while waving his arms like a rainbow.

As interested as Trina found herself, she didn't know if she should look too far into it. What did she look like uprooting her life in California and moving to cold ass Michigan? They get snow! But that condo and sunsets sounded quite intriguing.

"I haven't even seen the details of the job. What will I have to do?" She asked.

"It's quite similar to what you're doing now, just more flexibility and you work directly with the schools," Damon started. "It's an outreach coordinator position, where you will be overseeing the connections built with colleges and universities, local businesses, and community organizations to support the education of our students." He finished.

Trina was listening closely. As much as she didn't want to like it, something about the position sounded like she may like the change in scenery and diversify her resume.

"So, what about the superintendent?" Trina asked.

"He wants to meet with you briefly. If you want me to be honest, if he likes you, the job is basically yours. You'll be leaving here with a preliminary offer," he confidently said with a smile on his face.

"Good morning Ladies & Gentlemen, let's get this show on the road!" Yelled the host of the opening session.

Both Trina and Damon turned to face the front stage. Trina leaned in towards Damon and whispered, "You can set up the meeting. It won't hurt," and turned back to listen to the speaker.

The opening ceremony lasted about 45 minutes and included a keynote speaker who talked about the importance of stepping out of your comfort zone. "You will never know!" He kept repeating as he made each point. He sounded quite convincing.

Trina attended the 1st session of the day and received a message from Damon asking her to meet with him and Superintendent Samuels at 11:15 in the restaurant at their hotel. Trina replied back to his message and let him know that she would be there at 11:15. There was no response back to her confirmation.

The first session went by fast and Trina found herself slightly nervous for the lunch meeting she had planned with Damon and the Superintendent. After her session, she didn't dare stay for questions, she made her way across the street to her hotel and sat in the waiting area. It was 11:08am when she arrived, so they were expected to show up shortly. Trina pulled out her phone and sent Damon a text informing him that she was in the waiting area.

After a couple of minutes, Damon hadn't responded to her text yet. Shortly after she checked her phone, she noticed Damon appearing from inside the restaurant, motioning for Trina to follow him. They were already seated at a table in the back corner of the restaurant.

Trina had butterflies in her stomach the closer they got to the table. As they reached the table, Superintendent Samuels stood up, brushed off his suit, and reached his hand out to shake Trina's hand.

He had an aggressively tight squeeze of the hand as if he had no cares that she was a dainty feminine woman with freshly manicured nails.

After shaking her hand, he motioned for her to take a seat at the chair across from him.

"So, I hear a lot of good things about you Ms. Stansby, correct?" He asked before continuing. Trina gave him a head nod of approval and he continued talking. "Mr. Sylvestian tells me that you're interested in our new Outreach Coordinator position with the district?" He finished.

"Yes, this is correct," she answered.

"Now, from what he has told me, it sounds like you are amazing with making connections with people whom you have just recently met. Good with the networking skills, eh?" He asked with a smile on his face.

"Yes, I suppose you can say that Sir. I just find great value in meeting new people and finding ways we can help each other." Trina responded.

"And that, that is exactly what I like to hear!" Superintendent Samuels said as he sat up in his seat and looked over at Damon. "What makes you interested in switching to the education field, from the corporate world?" He asked.

"Well Mr. Samuels, If I'm to be honest..." Trina started...

"It's Dr. Samuels or Superintendent please," he corrected Trina.

"I apologize for that," Trina responded while clearing her voice and readjusting in her seat and crossing her leg. "Attending this conference this week has really opened my eyes up to the need for more people in the education field, more specifically in linking schools with reputable community organizations, college institutions, and the obtaining of resources that students feel are valuable for their current and future educational needs," Trina answered.

Superintendent Samuels nodded his head in agreement as Trina responded to his question. He seemed to be pleased with the impression she was making so far, as he had yet to stop smiling and showing his teeth every chance he got.

"Sounds like these conferences are still good for something!" He laughed out loud while hitting Damon on the back. Damon gave an uncomfortable grin and readjusted himself in his seat.

Trina looked back and forth from Damon to Dr. Samuels, trying to gauge the energy of the space and how it was really going.

"Did Mr. Sylvestian share with you the details of the position as well as the compensation package?" Superintendent Samuels asked.

Yes, sir. He shared with me the work expectations, salary range, and the purpose of creating the position," Trina responded. "This is a new position, correct?" She asked.

"Yes, this is correct. You will be the first person to start this position. The goal is to have a few people working under you to help with the workload in the next 2 years," Dr. Samuels responded.

"One of my questions would be, how much freedom do I have with the creation of this new department? Will I be allowed to help with the development of its policies and procedures?" Trina asked.

"Oh yes, we love when staff want to help with the creation of sustainability documents!" He said with excitement. "I think I want to hire you right now!" He laughed while his face turned red.

"Well, I think I'd be ready to sign the documents right now," Trina laughed back with Superintendent Samuels.

"You know what, there is something special about you that I just can't wrap my head around. I think I want to give you a preliminary offer for the position, how about that?" Superintendent Samuels asked.

"I think that sounds good, but I do have to ask about the benefits and compensation package in detail before I make a final decision," Trina responded.

"Oh no problem, I'll have the HR department reach out to you with any official information, but I can tell you that we come with full-coverage health insurance for you and up to 3 dependents. There are no co-pays and $0 deductibles. The offered salary is $100,000 with the chance of a 3% increase depending on your work during your probationary period of 6 months. To my understanding, you are in California correct?" He asked Trina.

"This is correct," she answered.

"So the package would come with a $10k relocation allowance and a full-service moving experience that's valued at an average of $7k. How does that sound?" He asked.

"With my experience in the corporate world and connection with many universities and organizations, as well as skill-set in the development of policies and procedures, I'd like to see that offer at $110k," Trina responded confidently.

"Since you have the ability to increase 3% after 6 months, and the other services you are utilizing, the most I can offer is $105k," Dr. Samuels responded, while sitting up in his seat.

Trina, while smiling, reached out her hand and Dr. Samuels grabbed it to shake.

"It looks like we have a deal, Dr. Samuels," she stated as they shook hands.

"Alrighty! I will have Mr. Sylvestian work on getting all of your details sent over to HR. They are going to reach out to go over formalized procedures for your hire. That should be around Wednesday when you hear something back," He stated, while glancing over at Damon briefly before looking at his watch. "Well won't you look at that! It's 11:35 already! Let's get some food in our bellies and finish talking over food," he finished as he reached for the menu in front of him.

The trio ordered and enjoyed their lunch in the likes of each other over laughs and glasses of wine. Trina really enjoyed herself and found herself slightly excited about accepting a position in a whole new city. She left lunch, went to the last session of the conference and showed her face at the closing ceremony.

That evening she and Damon had dinner with Dean Stringfew, Mr. Crenshee, and a few other pupils who were at the party the night before. Dinner was actually innocent as they spent over 80% of the time talking about their jobs, the tax law, and the scams of college. There was no sexual talk and Dean Stringfew didn't make not one advance towards her, like she expected her to. It was as if the night before hadn't even happened. No one talked about it and Trina wasn't going to be the one to break the ice.

By the end of dinner, she had exchanged contact information with everyone in attendance and they all promised to reach out and identify ways to work together with their individual work projects. Trina hadn't told them about her new job offer, but meeting them all felt like it was an on-time occasion and she wouldn't regret it in the future.

The rest of the conference went smoothly. After dinner, her and Damon met up for some R&R and a nightcap since both their flights left early Sunday morning. Damon made their last night together feel extremely comfortable and special as he had champagne and roses in the room awaiting her. Trina didn't want the moment to end and neither did Damon.

"I really enjoyed our time together this week," Damon told Trina once they finished making love for the last time.

Trina, smiling, responded "I really enjoyed myself too. I needed this."

"The same way I needed you?" Damon asked without thought.

'I guess you can say that," Trina snickered while playing with his chin.

"I hope you're serious about the job offer, I really feel like we are supposed to be in each other's life." Damon said while shifting his body to face her.

He kissed her on the forehead and started staring her in the eyes. Trina couldn't take the eye contact and immediately shifted her body and started glaring at the ceiling. "Say I agree to the job opportunity, you're not going to turn out to be crazy or anything are you?" She asked.

"No, why would I do that?" Damon asked.

"Because all of this is moving extremely fast. It is a little scary," she answered.

Damon turned Trina to face him. "If we are honest, I feel like you're my wife," he said.

"Wife?! I don't know if I'm ready for that one sir," Trina pulled away.

"I'm not asking you to marry me tomorrow, but I would like to see where it all goes. It's your world. Whatever you want, just name it and it's yours," Damon said while reaching to hold Trina near him again.

"I hear you hun. I hear you." Trina responded before turning to give him a kiss. They laid in the bed cuddling together until it was time for them to pack their things for their flight. Since both their flights left at 5am, they chose to ride to the airport together at 3.

Chapter 10: Poof! Now I'm Gone!

Trina's flight left on time at 5am, and she was so tired that she slept the entire flight. Thank goodness she was able to catch a direct flight and didn't have to worry about any connecting flights. Her flight landed at 7am local time, and it didn't take long for her to get her luggage and meet her driver at the airport pickup as arranged. Trina walked in the house at 9am and went straight to the shower and then bed. She didn't wake up until 3 in the afternoon, and that was because Damon was blowing up her phone.

"Hello..." Trina answered the phone half asleep.

"Did you make it? I hadn't heard from you," Damon responded.

"Babe, I'm so tired. I've been sleeping since I got home. I'mma talk to you later, ok?" Trina responded before ending the call. She didn't even wait for him to respond to her. She was so tired, none of it mattered. She rolled over and went back to sleep. He called her back and she was already a zombie asleep.

Trina didn't wake up until 7 that evening, when she finally felt like she had the energy to face the day. She took this time to unpack her suitcase, put a load of laundry in the washing machine, and cook dinner while catching up on emails. She had to be to work the next day bright and early at 8 in the morning. This meant her long nap was going to make it hard for her to go back to sleep and she didn't even care.

By 10, she had eaten, finished her laundry, and prepared for the next day. She wasn't expecting to be sleepy again, but to her surprise she was worn out and ready for bed again by 11 that night. Trina slept through the night with no problem and woke up at 5am ready to face the new week of work. She was expecting to get a phone call from the HR department by Wednesday and that was all she could find herself thinking about.

Trina walked into the office a little before 8am and it appeared she was the first person there. She went to the staff room, made a fresh brew of coffee, and made her way to her office. As soon as she got comfortable, her partner came bursting into her office without knocking, surprising Trina while she was taking a sip of her coffee.

"So, how was it?!" She asked.

"Well damn, Torie, you couldn't at least knock?" She asked while wiping the spilled coffee from her face and neck. "I almost ruined my blouse!"

"I'm so sorry girl! You need me to go get some soap and water? I have a tide wipe in my office," she asked as she turned to walk out the door.

"No, you're ok. It didn't make it to my blouse thank goodness," Trina responded.

"Cool! So, back to the question. I'm so sorry it got sprung on you last minute. It was some kind of stomach bug going around, it felt like I was dyyyyying!" Torie went on dramatically.

"I'm just glad you're feeling better girl," Trina said while rolling her chair to the other side of her desk. "It went really good. I made all of the connections that we needed with the universities. I have a few meetings set-up with them over the next week annnnnnd I met a man, girrrrl!" Trina said excitedly with a big smile on her face.

"Oop! Did Stella go over to Louisville and get her groove back? Tell me mooooore!" Torie said as she took a seat in the chair across from Trina and started sipping her tea.

"Girrrrrl!" Trina said with an even bigger grin on her face. "This man is everything! He opened my eyes up to a lot of things I hadn't thought about before."

Torie tilted her head, "and what was that?" She asked.

Trina started blushing, "Just his conversation and how he views the world. I feel like I could grow by knowing him."

"Listen, you deserve all the happiness that is coming your way. Definitely after that last asshole, you deserve peace and love!" Torie said with a huge smile on her face.

"Thank you for always being supportive, boo, I appreciate you," Trina smiled.

"You know I got you, love! Let me gone and get to work before Sharon start opening her mouth," Torie laughed as she got up from her seat. "I'll check back in a little later. Let me know if you need some help with those meetings," she finished as she made it to the doorway.

"I definitely will," Trina assured her.

Just as Torie walked out the door, Trina found herself looking out the window next to her desk.

There was a white butterfly fluttering near the rose bush. It was fluttering from rose to rose as if it was testing for the perfect landing. Trina smiled from a good place.

As soon as she turned back to the work on her desk, her cellphone started ringing. The number read 313-555-0110 from Detroit, MI. Trina already knew who it was. She jumped up, locked her office door and answered the phone by the 4th ring.

"Hello, this is Trina Stansby," she answered the phone.

"Good morning Ms. Stansby, this is Alex with the Depoint School district's Human Resources Department, is this a good time to talk?"

"Yes, this is the perfect time," Trina responded as she got comfortable in her seat.

"Great! So, your information was shared with me from Superintendent Samuels for the Coordinator position," Alex started talking. "I'm calling to go over financial and contact details. By the end of the conversation, if you are still interested, I'll have the contract sent over for you to sign within an hour of our conversation," Alex finished.

"Ok, that sounds great!" Trina responded.

"Perfect! So, before I begin, do you have any questions about the position they weren't able to answer during your interview?" Alex asked.

"No ma'am," Trina responded.

"Ok, great! If you find yourself having any questions during this conversation, feel free stop me. Even if it's mid sentence," she laughed.

Alex started talking about the position, the expectations, insurance benefit package, her moving stipend, and her potential start date. Trina found herself listening in amazement. She couldn't believe that she was about to uproot her life again and move to the midwest. The job came with amazing benefits that included all-inclusive health insurance with no deductibles and copays on top of a company credit card and first class flight benefits for her long distance work meetings since 50% of her time would be spent traveling.

Trina felt like this was the opportunity of a lifetime and said yes as soon as Alex asked her if she would formally accept the position. Her start date, July 21st, was exactly 1-month from the date of the conversation and 1-week before the teachers and administrators returned from summer break for orientation. It didn't take long for Alex to send her the contract after they got off the phone. By noon, she had returned her signed offer letter, typed her resignation letter, and delivered it personally to her boss.

"What is this?" Sharon asked as Trina handed her the letter.

"It's my resignation letter," Trina responded.

"You have to be kidding me? What do you mean by resignation letter? We are in the middle of an important transition and need you here!" Sharon started raising her trembling voice.

Trina kept a straight face as she sensed Sharon's emotions picking up. "I know Sharon, but a new opportunity presented itself and I'd be a fool to not take it," Trina responded.

"I knew I shouldn't have sent you to that conference. Something didn't feel right and I didn't listen to my gut!" She raised her voice even more. "Was it from the conference? Where are you going, what are they offering you?" She started asking without pause.

"Ms. Sharon, it honestly doesn't matter. Out of courtesy with the workload I decided to not-only tell you instead of using my PTO and never coming back, but I gave a 3-week's notice. That's more than enough time and respect," Trina said calmly.

Sharon stopped and thought for a moment. Trina had a point. She could've easily left them hanging in the middle of an important transition, but instead she decided to help as long as she could.

"What are they offering you, Stansby? I'm sure we can match it and beat it!" Sharon said confidently.

"Honestly, with the cost of living differences and salary range, I'd be making more than you and I'm sure HR isn't having that," Trina said with a slight smirk on her face.

Sharon was dumbfounded. She was speechless and couldn't say a word. Trina was right. She was making about $80,000 as her supervisor and there was no way HR was going to approve a hefty salary increase for someone who wasn't in a leadership position. Sharon sat looking into space for a moment. "You're right Trina. There's no way we would be able to fit that into our budget," she started. "Where are you going?" She asked.

Trina thought for a moment. "I'm moving to a new state," she responded. Something about her didn't trust telling Sharon where she was going too soon. She was the type of person who would try to sabotage someone's opportunity if it meant her winning in the end and Trina wasn't going for that.

Sharon looked at Trina sideways, "Well, I'm happy for you Stansby and wish you nothing but the best. We shal make due with the time we have left together." Sharon got the hint that Trina wasn't trying to give her too many details about her moving plans. She decided to retreat and Trina knew she wasn't really happy for her, but she just went along with it anyways.

The rest of the workday was awkward. Somehow, everyone in the office knew she was leaving before it was time for her to leave work for the day. It was damn near impossible for her to get anything done as people kept coming to her office like a revolving door. Trina knew they were all being nosey looking for information that she had no plans on giving them, but they continued to try anyway.

She didn't have a problem with them until Torie came to her office pouting with an attitude, right when she was packing up for the day.

"Uh uh! Sit yo ass down! So you were going to sit here this morning and not tell me that you got a new job offer?!" She demanded.

"Well, first off, it wasn't official until after we talked and 2nd of all, you know you have a hard time holding water if I'm to be honest right now," Trina responded.

Torie didn't say anything for a few moments. She looked at Trina with her lip puffed up showing that she had an obvious attitude. "I just thought we were better than that! You're really just going to get up and leave?!" She asked.

"Listen, at the end of the day, if it was you, you would be doing the same thing." Trina said as she grabbed her things and walked towards the door. "We can finish talking about it another day, right now I'm tired as hell and don't have the energy," she finished as she walked out the door; leaving Torie with her mouth wide open staring at her walking away.

That entire evening, Trina spent time researching condos in Detroit and sizing up her home to see what she was going to take with her and what was going to stay. She hadn't even told Kisha that she was leaving yet. It was going to break her, but Trina knew she would understand at the end of the day. Plus, it would give her a new place to visit when she needed to get away from her kids and husband.

As soon as she closed her laptop for the night, She picked up her phone to call Kisha. Her and the family had just gotten in from their trip and she sounded tired as hell.

"Hey girl! How does it feel to be back after getting some dick?" Kisha asked while laughing.

Trina laughed with her, "It feels so good that I accepted a job offer in Michigan. I'm moving in 3 weeks!"

Kisha got quiet and there was an awkward silence that Trina didn't know how to manage. "Hey girl, did you hear me?" She asked Kisha.

"Yea, I heard you. But I'm trying to figure out what you mean by you accepted a new job position. What is that supposed to mean? You are moving for a man you just met?!" She asked like an angry mama who just found out her daughter was pregnant by a dusty bum. "I know I said you should look into it, but I wasn't serious. At least not this soon Sis!"

"I wouldn't say it's for a man. I'd say it's more of an opportunity that was hard to say no to. With an almost $40,000 pay increase on top of other bonuses, I think it's actually worth it." Trina responded. She paused to see if Kisha would respond. When she was silent for a few seconds, Trina continued talking. "On top of that, I won't have to worry about my living expenses and I doubt he would do anything stupid since he has such a high ranking job," she finished explaining herself.

"I really don't understand you. I don't know about this one Trina. I think you need to think about this a little longer," Kisha responded.

"I promise this will be good for me boo. I promise! Plus, now you will have somewhere else you can visit for vacations, remember you said that yourself!" Trina said in an attempt to brighten Kisha's mood. It wasn't helping. Kisha kept going silent and the tone of her voice when she talked showed exactly how she felt. At this point, Trina didn't feel confident telling her that Damon was going to be paying for her living expenses while she transitioned. She was sure Kisha was going to start calling her a sugar baby at that point. Which is actually what she would've thought if one of her friends told her the same thing.

Kisha wasn't having it and her mood changed drastically. "Girl, I'm about to get these kids taken care of. I'm happy you made it safely. We can catch up later," she said before ending the call. She didn't even wait for Trina to respond to her, she basically ended the call in her face.

Trina's transition was a lot of work to manage. She was able to find housing a week later, she secured her move date, and the movers had her packed up a day before her move. It seemed like no one from her home was happy about her transition to Michigan. Everyone around her felt like it was a bad move to make except Damon. He called her at least once, most times twice, a day to make sure everything was going well. He kept his word about her housing and gave her the money for her condo's first 3-months rent upfront. He seemed to be more excited about her moving than she was.

Her job was very awkward her last three weeks there. It seemed like people weren't talking to her as much, she was no longer invited to various staff meetings, and was made to feel like an outsider. Everything that was happening made her even more excited to move. She knew in her heart it was the best decision she could have made. When it came to moving day, Trina had everything ready to go and of course no one wanted to see her off. She hadn't talked to Kisha since the day she told her she was moving. Everytime she tried calling her, she'd either send her to voicemail or have one of her kids answer the phone and say she was busy. Trina even tried popping up at her house and Kisha didn't bother to open the door. She acted like she wasn't home, but Trina knew she was.

Life was changing and Trina was ready for the new beginning. If her life could change so drastically in the matter of less than a month, the sky was the limit for the rest of her life. Trina decided to have her car towed with the moving company and caught her flight shortly after the moving crew started on the road.

Chapter 11: New Beginnings

It was a beautiful Monday afternoon when she landed in Detroit. The sun was out and the sky was a clear blue with no clouds in sight. Damon picked her up from the airport as promised, meeting her with flowers, an Escalade truck, and food. If no one else was happy for her move, he was.

"Hey Baby girl!" He said with the biggest smile on his face, as he went in for the sloppiest kiss known to mankind. By the time he was done, Trina had his saliva all on her chin and above her lip. She didn't like it, but she knew it was because he was happy to see her so she let it slide that time.

When they stopped embracing, he handed Trina her flowers and led her to the truck. The driver placed her bags in the trunk of the car and they were on their way to get the keys to her place. They didn't waste any time in the truck. As soon as the driver started off, they closed the partition and within 60 seconds her dress was up, his pants were down, and they were in sexual bliss. Trina didn't care about the driver and neither did Damon. They were fucking so hard, the car was moving from side to side as they drove along the highway.

"Ohhh baby, I missed being inside you so much!" Damon moaned. "Now, I got you whenever I want you," he continued as he pumped harder and harder, forcing Trina to moan louder with each stroke.

"Oooh zaddy! Fuck me please. I need it!" Trina begged him.

This just made him harder. He pulled her titties out of her dress and started biting her nipples as he dove deeper and deeper inside of her. Trina couldn't hold in the pleasure she was receiving and next thing she knew she was cumming solely off dick, which usually never happened. "Baby, I'm cumming!" She screamed!

"Oooh, cum for me baby, please!" Damon begged. He pulled his dick out of her and got on his knees. He started sucking on her clit like he was trying to drink all of her juices until there was nothing left inside of her. She could no longer feel her legs, as they shook uncontrollably. She grabbed his head and started moving it up and down, pushing his face deeper into her coochie. There was nothing he could do, but oblige to her directions.

"You missed me?" He asked as he came up for air?

"You know I did!" She moaned.

"Is this my pussy now?" He asked her the next time he came up for air.

"You know it is!" She responded without thinking. At this point Trina was in a trance and so was Damon. A connection she had never had but was excited to experience.

They fucked in the back of the truck until they pulled up to her condo. It wasn't until the Driver stopped when they realized where they were. That was the quickest 30 minute drive they had ever experienced. As soon as the car stopped, they started scrambling to get their close together and look presentable. They failed horribly at the task. Damon's shirt was tucked in wrong. His pants were still unzipped. Trina's hair was all out of place and her dress looked like it had stretched 2 sizes bigger. They got each other together as much as possible, before walking into the building. They looked and smelled like sex. Anyone in their right mind would be able to tell, but they didn't give a fuck about it.

The leasing office of her new condo was absolutely beautiful! It was decorated like a jungle oasis and had a water fountain in the middle of the lobby and a wide opening that allowed you to see up to the pool on the 5th floor.. There was a restaurant on one end of the foyer and mini grocery store and shopping center on the other. It was like its own little city inside of a building. Trina knew she had made the right decision as soon as she walked in. She had already done most of the logistics before coming, so all she had to do was pay the rest of her fees and get her keys. The entire process took about 1 hour to complete. Once she was done, the leasing agent gave her a tour of the building and showed her to her new home.

The building turned out to be even more beautiful than her first impression. There was a garden in the back of the building and butterfly sanctuary that was enclosed for weather purposes. A stocked lake was outside the garden area and had a beautiful view with a waterfall. The water was crystal clear. There was a pool on the 5th floor of the building with a glass bottom. Below the glass was an enclosure with artificial flowers, plants, and animals like they were in a jungle. Trina's home was on the 15th floor, which was the top floor of the building. When she walked in, she was absolutely amazed at her view and the energy of the space. She had glass windows lined from the ceiling to the floor across her entire wall, facing the Detroit River and Canada.

This is the life, she thought to herself as she got a tour of her new home.

"Welcome to Detroit!" Damon yelled with a huge smile on his face. "May you make many memories and feel like the Queen you are," he said before giving her a kiss on the cheek.

Trina decided to stay the night at Damon's since her items weren't going to arrive until the next day. Little did she know, he didn't stay too far from her. It was like they were basically neighbors. His home faced the Detroit River as well. It wasn't as upgraded as hers, but you could tell that it cost a pretty penny to live there. They stayed up all night laying on the floor, in front of the floor length windows looking out into the night sky talking to each other about everything. Trina felt like she had found her forever home and Damon felt like he found his forever in her.

Trina's mover's didn't make it until late the next night. It was dark outside, so they decided to sleep and move all of her items in the house. By Wednesday afternoon, Trina was all moved in and she rushed to get everything unpacked. One thing she hated was having an unorganized home, so it was a no go to have boxes sitting around her house for months. It took her 3 days to get everything unpacked and put into their respective places. Damon helped her everyday when he got off work with the heavy duty items; all of the things she didn't want to deal with.

By the time everything was all in place, it was Saturday night and she had to start getting ready for her first day of work on Monday. Trina was nervous and slightly scared, but she knew it would all work out for her in the end. That didn't stop her from having mini panic attacks all day Saturday and Sunday though. Thankfully, she had Damon there to comfort her through the anxiety that kept taking over her body.

It was now Sunday night and Trina was laying on the couch in front of Damon. He had his arms wrapped around her as they laid there looking out the window at the water.

"Life is such an interesting thing," Trina said out of nowhere. "Just when we feel like we have it all figured out, we are put in a situation where we are forced to change something once again," she finished.

"I know right! I thought I wanted to be a firefighter and look at me now," Damon laughed.

"It's like, never had I ever thought I would be living in Michigan among all of the places in the world. It was never on my radar," Trina continued.

Damon kissed Trina on the top of her head, "Thank goodness I saw you in the airport that day."

"Yea…" Trina said with a hesitation before tilting her head to look into Damon's eyes. "It definitely feels like it was fated to happen."

"You're going to do great at your job babe, don't worry, I promise," Damon assured her while turning her body to look at him. "I know good people when I see them and you're not good. You're amazing!

Always know that!" He inflected his voice before kissing her passionately.

Damon and Trina found themselves making love on the rug in front of the window. So passionate, Damon treated Trina like she was a Queen. He kissed and loved on every part of her body as if he was blessing her with the gifts of confidence and trust. By the time they were done, Trina knew she found the man for her. He spoke to her soul in ways no man had ever spoke to her soul before. He assured her more than she'd ever received from another. When she was with him she felt like she could do, and have, anything. He brought the balance that she never knew she needed.

Trina stayed over Damon's Sunday night and they left for work at the same time. As she trailed him to the office, she looked at the scenery along the way. From the trees to the flowers, to the people on the street she learned that Detroit was such a diverse city that just may have a lot to offer her. It took them about 25 minutes to get from their home to the office base she would be working at. It was a 3-story brick building that looked like it was due for an upgrade. On the outside of the building was a large sign in the front that read "Welcome to the Depoint Board of Education: Where learning is the priority and laziness is prohibited." Trina laughed as they got closer to the sign and entrance to the building.

"What are you laughing at?" Damon asked.

"That saying on the sign. I've never seen anything like that before, posted outside such an important establishment," she answered.

"That sign has been there since this building was constructed back in the 60's. Don't let the ratchetness scare you away, it's been time for an upgrade" he laughed as he opened the door for Trina to enter.

Trina walked through the double doors into the foyer of the building. It had high ceilings and a receptionist desk planted in the middle of the room. To the right were a spiral staircase leading to the 2nd level of the building. To the right was an older looking elevator that Trina didn't expect to use often. It looked like plenty of people had spent their share of time being stuck inside. It appeared that Damon had similar thoughts because after he checked in with the receptionist, he went straight to the stairs and didn't even flash a glance towards the elevator.

"How many people have been stuck in that thing?" Trina asked while pointing at the elevator.

"Too many to count," he laughed from a joyful place and kept walking up the stairs.

"I bet!" She laughed.

When they made it to the 2nd floor, Damon led Trina down a hallway with blue carpet. There were a few visible stains she passed along the way before they made it to a room on the right. The room had a window in the far corner that allowed a great deal of light to shine through. The light reflected off the mirror placed on the opposite side of the office, which then reflected onto the bookcase. There was hardwood flooring, a large work desk in the middle of the floor, 2 chairs and a couch.

"This is going to be your office, Ms. Stansby," Damon said as he guided her into the room. "You can set your items over there on the shelf, as I show you around the office and give you a chance to meet with Superintendent Samuels," he continued as he pointed to the shelf on the east end of the room. "He has set a 9am meeting with you to start your onboarding process. Then, you will be training with me until lunch. After lunch, you will meet with Anita, in the technology department to get your laptop, technology user information, and other technical things that I know about," he let out a nervous giggle.

Trina looked down at her watch. It was 8:15am and she had 45 minutes until she was set to meet with Superintendent Samuels.

"So, what are we going to do for the next 45 minutes?" She asked.

"Well, you can walk around the building and do some sight seeing... not that there is alot to see," Damon answered.

"Or..." Trina said, while looking over at the couch along the wall and looking back at him.

"What are you trying to say?" Damon asked with a smirk, as if he didn't already know what she was talking about.

"You know what I'm talking about!" Trina said sarcastically.

"Baby, we are at work right now. I'm freaky, but I've never done something like that before," Damon said with an element of fear in his voice.

"Take a seat," Trina said as she guided Damon to the couch. She closed the office door, locked it, and walked over to Damon. "I know Mr. Confident Big

Daddy Dick Thrower isn't afraid to take care of Mama at work?" Trina asked.

"It's not that I'm afraid it's just that I like to keep work and my personal life private," Damon said as Trina got down on her knees. She started trying to unbuckle his belt, but he started scrambling to make her stop. "No baby, not right now. We can wait until we get home," he finished as he pushed Trina away.

As soon as he got her away, he stood up, fixed his pants, and opened the office door.

"I'm going to go check-in with my secretary and I'll be back around 8:45 to take you to Superintendent Samuels' office," Damon said as he walked out the door and closed it.

Trina sat there looking dumbfounded. *Did he just turn me down?* Trina asked herself as she looked at the closed door in front of her. She stood there looking at the door in disgust, confused.

Trina snapped out of it and walked over to her desk. As soon as she took a seat, there was a knock at the door. "Come in!" Trina yelled at the door.

As the door opened, a short black woman with blonde hair and red lipstick appeared. "Heeeeeey Girrrrl!! Welcome to the team!" She yelled with a high pitched voice. "My name is Ashley, I work in the K-6 curriculum department, what's your name again?" She asked while reaching her hand out for a handshake.

"My name is Trina Stansby, nice to meet you Ashley...?" Trina responded.

"Oh, sorry about that girl, it's Ashley Lane. I forgot they said your name was Trina! I was so hype cause all I could think about was the Baddest Bih!" Ashley said with her lips pouted, head tilted to the side, and booty poked out like she was about to burst into a twerk.

Trina laughed, "Yea, that's my name."

"Well, welcome to the district girl. I need to get back to this meeting, just wanted to stop in and say hi. Let's have lunch sometime this week!" She said as she walked backwards out of the door.

"Sounds Good!" Trina said as she sat down in her chair.

Oh, this is going to be really interesting, Trina thought to herself.

She got up and walked over to the window. Outside of the window was the view of a small lake surrounded by trees, flowers, ducks and geese. It was a beautiful view that she could get used to for sure.

It didn't take long for 8:45am to roll around. Damon came walking in her office without knocking as soon as the clock turned. "Are you ready Ms. Stansby?" He asked.

Trina looked at him sideways, grabbed her purse, and stood up to follow him.

"How is it going so far?" He asked.

Trina looked at him, rolled her eyes, and said yes like she had the biggest attitude in the world. *Did he really think I was going to move on from that, that fast?* She thought to herself as they walked down the hall towards the stairs. Damon led Trina down the stairs, past the receptionist desk, and down a hallway next to the elevator. They walked all of the way down the hallway and stopped at a door located at the end. The door to the office didn't look like the others. It had a newly painted oak door, with a gold handle and name plate over the top that read: *Dr. Samuels, Superintendent.*

Damon knocked on the door three times and someone immediately instructed him to open the door and come inside. Damon opened the door slowly, peeking his head in as he walked in further. "Good morning Dr. Samuels! I have Ms. Stansby here for your 9am meeting, is this still a good time?" Damon asked in a submissive tone.

"Oh of course, come on in!" He said excitedly as he got up from his seat to greet them. Dr. Samuels reached his hand out to Trina for a handshake, "Good morning Ms. Stansby, I hope you are liking the energy of the office so far."

"Yes, it's been nice so far. I had a chance to meet Ms. Lane, she seems really nice," Trina said.

Dr. Samuels cleared his throat and straightened his suit, "yes, we are definitely a family here!" He said with a smile on his face. "Thank you so much for escorting Ms. Stansby to me Mr. Sylvestian. Are you still able to come back at 10?" Dr. Samuels asked.

"Oh, yes for sure. I'll be back at 10am on the dot! You two have a great meeting," Damon responded before turning and walking out the door.

"Have a seat Ms. Stansby," Dr. Samuels said while directing her to a chair on the other side of his desk.

Trina sat down in the chair and placed her purse in the chair that was next to her. They spent the next hour going over the district policies, the history of the school district, the areas he feels there is the most need, and details surrounding the back to school orientation schedule. The rest of the day was spent with Damon training her on coordinator duties, showing her around the office, and he introduced her to everyone in the office. After lunch, Trina met with the technology manager, received her work computer, email details, and school links and passwords.

The rest of the week consisted of her finishing her onboarding process, preparing her orientation details for the school principals, completing HR paperwork, and getting acclimated to the new atmosphere. She had no choice but to jump in head first. She didn't have a choice. She was now managing an entire department and felt like she had a lot of pressure on her to show up with 1000% percent.

Trina had an attitude with Damon for the rest of the week because of what happened. He had flowers sent to her home everyday with the purpose of apologizing, but Trina wasn't having it. She found herself throwing them one by one down the garbage disposal as she scrolled through social media. *He got me fucked up,* she thought to herself as she'd scroll looking at fine black men on beaches, in gyms, and in their hoochie daddy shorts.

"It wouldn't be hard to find another one," Trina said out loud as she got up from the couch to shower and get ready for bed. It was the night before the first day of orientation with her job and she wanted to be fully rested for the work that was ahead of her. When she finished showering, she turned her phone on **Do Not Disturb,** laid her clothes out for the next day, and opened her blinds to allow the moonlight to shine through until she fell asleep.

Cheers to new beginnings, she thought to herself as she drifted to sleep like a baby who had just finished sucking on a titty.

Chapter 12: Harpo, who dis man??

Trina arrived at the Board of Education 30 minutes before the group session met. The first day of orientation was with all of the school principals, directors and coordinators. Just as she parked her car, Damon was pulling into his designated parking spot. Trina kept walking like she hadn't seen him. *He's not dumb enough to cause drama at work*, she thought to herself as she let herself into the front door.

"Good morning! Welcome to Day 1 of Orientation! You can sign in over there," The welcoming assistant said as she pointed to the table next to her. "We have complementary bagels, coffee, and fruit downstairs in the foyer, before you walk into the meeting space," she finished with a big smile on her face. Trina nodded and flashed back a smile as she moved to the next table, trying hard to not look towards the door. It was like her coochie could feel him behind her.

As soon as Trina finished signing in and writing her name tag, she turned around and **bloop**! Her and Damon clashed into each other like their first encounter in the elevator.

"Oh, I'm sorry Ms. Stansby. Let me get that for you..." He said as he pretended there was something on her face as he brushed her cheek with this thumb. "That should be better," he said as he moved over to sign in for the day. Trina stood there for a few seconds before getting her composure and heading downstairs to the meeting room. It was something about him that still got her wet, and all she could do was thank God that she wore a dark colored dress for the day. If she hadn't she was sure it would look like she had peed on herself.

The meeting room was filling up as everyone started to make their way in with their danishes and coffee. Some had their own coffee and others used the office cups. Either way it went, everyone had a cup in their hand and it was only the first day back. Trina took a seat at the table located in the back corner, near the 2nd door. She didn't want to run the risk of Damon sitting next to her and she honestly wanted to observe everyone else first. She wasn't a Detroit native and had heard that Detroit natives were a different breed. She preferred to observe.

Once 9am hit, the room was 80% full with about 120 people minimum. Just as she thought she was lucky to not have anyone sit next to her, here came a shorter light skinned man plopping down into the seat. Trina took a glance over at him before looking at the empty seats in front of her. *Now he know he could've sat up there*, she thought to herself as he rummaged through this briefcase, pulling out papers.

He was light skinned with a beard connecting from both sides of cheek. He had thick eyebrows and a low cut that looked freshly lined. He smelled like coconut mango butter with hazel eyes that matched perfectly.

"Good morning, sorry for making all of this noise," he leaned over and whispered to Trina while flashing his perfectly white teeth.

Trina's disdain quickly vanished as she took in more of his scent. He smelled like magic. "Oh, no, I totally understand," Trina said with a giggle as she motioned her hand in a half wave. She was obviously flirting and wasn't doing a good job of it.

"I'm Trina Stansby, the new Outreach Coordinator of recruitment for the district," she said as she reached her hand out for a shake.

"Nice to meet you," He said as he grabbed her hand. "My name is Mr. Quinn, the Principal at Elmwood High on the westside," he finished before letting her hand go.

Trina had to catch herself as she barely heard what he said as she took in the feel of his hand. It's like she felt his energy shoot through her like a shock wave. "It's nice to meet you, Mr.Stinn?" she asked.

He laughed and bit his bottom lip, "Mr. Quinn is better."

"What about Mr. Q?" She asked with a big smile on her face. "I feel like I may mess it up again," she finished as she let out a giggle.

They both laughed before Dr. Samuels started talking at the front of the room. Mr. Quinn turned his chair to face the front of the room like the commander had just called his soldiers to attention.

"Good morning, Team!" Dr. Samuels said as he started pacing the room. "Welcome back for the 2022-2023 school year! I'm so excited to see all of your faces today!" He continued with a big smile on his face. He had on a dark green suit with a white and baby blue tie for the district colors. It was a little corny, but it was cute at the same time. "To start the day, we are going to have Mr. Sylvestian lead us through the agenda today," He finished as he motioned for Damon to take over the lead. Trina shifted in her seat as she found herself upset, yet horny at the same time. Mr. Quinn looked at Trina as she bumped him on accident, with her purse hanging on her seat, while shifting in her seat.

"Good morning everyone!" Damon said as he received a good morning in return from half the room. "Oh no no no. We can't start the day like that y'all. GOOD MORNING!" He yelled across the room.

"GOOD MORNING!" Everyone yelled back; including Trina.

"Ok nah, that is much better! You had me scared at first," he laughed as he fixed his suit. "So today before we get started, we are going to do a quick icebreaker with the person next to you. It's called, "Tell Us A Story!" How you play is, you and the person next to you, or someone else if they stink," everyone laughed. "You get 5 minutes to make up a story to tell everyone from information you both connect to. When the time is up, I'm going to randomly select names from this list to tell their story!" He finished excitedly. "The instructions are pretty straightforward, but do we have any questions?" He asked. He looked around the room to find that no one had their hand up with a question. "Alright, begin!" He directed everyone.

Trina and Mr. Quinn turned and looked at each other. "I guess this means you're my partner now," he said with a laugh while looking around.

"Yea, I guess so," Trina smiled. "So, we have to talk about something we can both relate to… huhm… what's your favorite movie?" She asked.

"I don't know if I want to share that with you yet," he laughed.

"What is it? Stop playing," Trina laughed back with him.

"If I tell you, I don't want to hear any laughing; ok?" He asked as he made a serious, yet joking face. He couldn't hold it for long before laughing again. As she was laughing, Damon walked by as if he was looking to see how their pair was doing.

"Looks like the icebreaker is going along really well," he said as he passed by Trina and Mr. Quinn. "Can't wait to potentially hear your story," he finished before walking to the next group.

Trina caught herself from rolling her eyes, and focused back on Mr. Quinn. "Ok, Ok, I know I'm laughing right now, but I promise I won't judge you!" She assured him.

"Ok, Ok. My favorite movie is actually the Harry Potter series from beginning to end. I can spend a whole day binge watching one through eight, repeating every word," he laughed.

"Boyyyy, that's my favorite movie too! Now, what really matters is what house you're in, cause if I don't like it, we can't be friends," she said.

"Oh dang, you're not even going to give me a chance, huh?" He asked with his head tilted and lip bit.

"What house are you in?" Trina asked.

"I'm actually Ravenclaw, you?" He responded.

"Well look at that, we are in the same house," she answered with a smile. "We can be good friends after all," she finished.

"Alright, so how about we recreate a story from one of the movies, with our own characters?" Mr. Quinn asked.

"I like where you're going with it," Trina nodded her head up and down.

"How about the scene where Malfoy stupified Harry and left him on the train? But then Luna came and noticed him?" He asked.

Trina started getting hype, "That would be perfect! We could make it as if you are a student who feels invisible and left out, but then Luna comes and sees through you!" She was getting really excited! "Well, not you as Luna. I can be Luna and you can be Harry," she finished.

"I actually like that alot!" Mr. Quinn responded with the same excitement as her. "It feels like we are approaching our 5-minutes, you want to just wing it if we are called?" He asked.

"I'm down," Trina said back with a smile. "I know that movie up and down and I'm sure we'd vibe with the flow," she finished.

Mr. Quinn smiled at her.

"Alright everyone, that's your 5- minutes. If you're not done, that's fine. It was a last minute exercise anyways," Damon said jokingly. "Alright, I'm going to randomly pick 2 names and those groups are going to share their skit, cool?" Damon asked before the crowd replied back with a "cool!"

Trina thought her and Mr. Quinn would get called, but unfortunately their masterpiece had to stay between them along with their mutual adoration for Harry Potter. They were lowkey geeks, and Trina loved every bit of it. After they finished the icebreaker, Damon went over the agenda with the group. They were going to get details about the new regulations affecting the district, celebrated the employees with major milestones in the district, created district and school goals, and mix & mingled until about 1pm. Mr. Quinn and Trina had basically worked together the whole day and their vibe was undeniable. It was something about him that she wanted.

When lunch time came around, Trina got up to head to her office.

"Aye, hold up real quick Trina!" Mr. Quinn yelled after her as she walked up the hallway towards the stairs.

Trina turned around with a smile on her face, "What's up?" She asked as Mr. Quinn caught up to her.

"I was wondering if you wanted to go to lunch with me? Since you're new, give you a chance to experience something different," he suggested.

Trina had no plans for lunch and thought, *what the heck*, as she shrugged in response. "Where are you trying to take me?" She asked him as they walked up the stairs.

"We have this place called Coney Island. Best food ever, especially when you're hung over or have the munchies," he laughed. "You haven't received a welcome to Detroit until you've had a Coney!" He said hyped up.

As they reached the top of the stairs, Trina spotted Damon near the receptionist desk and made sure to make eye contact with him as she and Mr. Quinn walked out the building together. Mr. Quinn lead Trina to a black Mercedes-Benz with tinted windows. He opened her door and ran to the driver's side of the car.

Trina looked around his car subtly. The interior was red and black leather with a diamond engraved on the dash. It was clean and smelled like candied cinnamon apples. Trina would've never thought a man drove his car if she hadn't witnessed it herself first.

Mr. Quinn hopped in the car, put on his seatbelt and raised his body towards the steering wheel before reversing out of his parking spot. He had his right elbow on the seat and his left hand on the steering wheel.

As they pulled out of the parking lot, Trina's phone started ringing. She looked down at her phone to see that it was Damon calling her. She immediately sent him to voicemail without making it obvious. Trina's phone started vibrating a couple of minutes later. She looked down at her phone, to see she had a notification from Damon. She opened the text message and started reading.

Oh, so you're going to lunch with people you just met? What if I wanted to go to lunch with you? The text message read. For some reason, Trina found herself tickled by Damon's text. How dare he say something about what she did for lunch. If he wanted to go to lunch with her, he would've said something before seeing her with someone else.

"Everything ok over there?" Mr. Quinn asked as he glanced over at Trina, looking at her phone first and then her.

"Oh yea, everything is fine. A friend was asking me a question," she answered. "Anyways, what type of music do you like to listen to? Put something on for me," Trina changed the subject.

"Oh, you ready for some of that Detroit music?" Mr. Quinn asked while picking up his phone and scrolling through his music. He turned on an upbeat song with a heavy baseline. "Listen, once you get into the real Detroit, you're going to be stuck," he said while biting his lip and putting his eyes back on the road. He started nodding his head as the artist came on with a smooth flow. It was like he was rapping at one speed while the music was going another tempo. Even with the differences, it's like it went together perfectly.

"Oh, I like this!" Trina said as she nodded her head to the music. "So, do you like R&B too? I'm an R&B type of girl." She asked.

"Oh yea, I love to get my love on!" He laughed. "How about you connect your bluetooth and share some music with me."

It took Trina a couple of minutes to get her bluetooth going, but once she started playing music, it was like they were having a concert in a stadium. They both were in the car nodding their heads to the music, glancing at each other from time to time, and giving some smart remarks to the other as a way to be funny. They were moving and grooving, as they made their way to food.

When they pulled up to the restaurant, it looked nothing like how Trina had envisioned it to look like. She thought they would be going to a new establishment in a nice neighborhood, the way he was talking. The restaurant had bulletproof glass surrounding the windows and work area. Trina noticed bullet holes in the drive thru window next to the front door as they walked to the front door. There were blighted buildings surrounding, making Trina feel less safe.

I don't know if I'm safe here, Trina thought to herself as he held the door open for her. She walked in slowly while looking around the establishment. It looked like the lobby hadn't been mopped in two months of Sundays, the cooks were dressed in their work attire with 9mm's on their waist, the cashier had on a 2-piece velour outfit with a butterfly belly ring and 2-inch nails to go with it.

Trina looked at the menu and decided to go with the grilled chicken salad. Mr. Quinn ordered 2 coney dogs and a large chili cheese fry. It didn't take long for the food to be done, so they sat down and ate there before heading back to the training. Trina had never had a salad taste as good as her salad tasted. It was loaded with grilled chicken, banana peppers, tomatoes, cucumbers, jalapenos, cheese and grilled peppers with a homemade ranch dressing. Trina was in heaven and instantly started repenting for judging the business.

"Is this black owned?" Trina asked as she put another bite of salad in her mouth.

"I don't know if they are black-owned, but I know I have only seen black people working in here my whole life," Mr. Quinn laughed while wiping chili off the side of his lips.

Once they finished their food, they made their way back to the training. The rest of the day went by pretty fast and Trina and Mr. Quinn found themselves hitting it off pretty good. Before they left for the day, he made sure to exchange phone numbers with Trina in the case they had to "do some work together." Trina knew he wanted her phone number for more than work, but she let him take the lead the way he chose.

When Trina made it back home, she was greeted by a dozen roses and a gourmet seafood meal at the front desk for her. She already knew who it was from and at that point, she was ready to forgive him and move on. When she made it upstairs to her condo, she called Damon and he answered on the first ring.

"Hey baby, you make it home yet?" He asked.

"Yes, I'm sure you already knew that though," Trina said as she took her heels off and took them to her room.

"I'm really sorry baby and I miss you alot," Damon said, as he sat in his car, still in the parking lot of the Board of Education.

"I miss you too. You should come over," Trina told him as she undressed in front of the mirror. "I'm taking off my clothes now, and need someone to wash my back," she said with a soft mellow voice.

"I'll be there in 20," Damon said while reversing his car out of the parking spot.

"Ok babe," Trina responded before they both hung up the phone.

Trina was horny after her interaction with Mr. Quinn all day and since she couldn't have him, Damon was better than her vibrator for the night.

I honestly wish I could have both of them, Trina thought to herself as she touched herself in the mirror.

When she finished analyzing her body in the mirror, she went back into the kitchen and started eating the food Damon sent her. It was a seafood feast with lobster, King crab legs, shrimp, crawfish, a baked potato, and salad. Seafood was her absolute favorite food and Damon knew exactly what he was doing when he bought it. She dug in and as soon as her hands got good and dirty, Damon was knocking on the door.

"One minute!" Trina yelled at the door as she rinsed and dried her hands on the dish towel. When she made it to the door, she looked through the peep and then opened the door. Damon burst through the door and started kissing Trina all over her forehead, cheeks, and neck. It was like he had been starving himself for weeks and she was his intended fasting meal. As he sucked on her neck, she felt her knees get weak as the sensation ran through her blood vessels.

Trina pulled away from Damon's embrace and walked back into the kitchen. "You want some babe?" Trina asked as she started back cracking her crab legs.

"No thank you, I'm still full from lunch," Damon responded. "Speaking of lunch, you and Mr. Quinn was getting kind of close today," he finished.

Trina looked at him with a blank expression before saying, "ok?"

"I'm just saying. You're not about to replace me already are you?" He asked with a nervous laugh. "I mean, I'll still keep my obligation to pay for your condo, but don't be out here trying to replace me," he finished.

Trina got up off the island stool and walked over to Damon. With her hands holding both sides of his face, she kissed him two times and said, "Baby, you will always be my number one," and went back to her stool and food.

Damon stopped talking after that, and Trina didn't ask any questions. He made himself comfortable in the living room until she finished eating. When she got done, they both showered together in her walk-in shower where they made love passionately against the wall and on the floor of the shower. The feeling of the water hitting their body made the sex feel 10x better as she rode him on the shower floor. It was like they were both fish, because the water was the last thing on their mind.

Damon grasped the side of the wall as Trina rode him faster and faster. The water of the shower was hitting his face like it was trying to drown him and all he could think about was making sure she got the pleasure she needed.

A few minutes later, Damon was at a place where it was hard to retain himself. "Baby, I'm about to cum!" He shouted as Trina gripped her pussy around his dick as she rode back and forth. "Baby, I'm about to cum!" He repeated himself. Trina didn't get off like she usually did when he was about to cum.

"Do you want to cum in me tonight daddy?" Trina asked in a playful tone. Before he could answer, he shot his load deep inside of her and she could feel it like water was traveling up her coochie canal. "Ooooh baby, your cum feels so good inside of me," Trina said as she rolled around on his dick, still riding him.

"Thank you for letting me cum inside of you baby. You know that's what I've been wanting," he struggled to say as his eyes rolled in the back of his head. Trina got off his dick and started sucking him and her juices off his magic stick. "Baby, we taste so good together," Trina said as she finished sucking. Damon's toes were curled and he was laying there like a log. He was frozen in pleasure and Trina felt like the Queen of the castle.

Damon stayed over that night and got dressed at Trina's since he had a few suits already at her place.

Chapter 13: Call me by my name

The rest of the training went along smoothly. Trina and Mr. Quinn found themselves flirting more and more as each day went by, finding a way to be near each other and communicate. Their communication continued once the training was over. They went from talking about Harry Potter to the school year, to eventually having their first official date a couple of months later. During that time of talking, Trina learned that Mr. Quinn's given name was Evan which made her give him the nickname, EQ. He also had a 6 year old son from his previous relationship whom he had shared custody with. Between running a school and being a dad, it was a lot for them to navigate when it came to time.

It was the first week of October when EQ and Trina had their first date. He wanted their date to be a surprise, so he told her to dress casually and he picked her up at 3pm on the Saturday before Fall Break. They started their date at a Butterfly conservatory on the Eastside of the city. Trina had been living in the city for a few months and hadn't learned that there was a butterfly conservatory, but she was beyond excited to finally experience it. EQ learned that Trina loved butterflies from their conversations and clearly he was taking notes, because after their date with the butterflies he had a picnic set up along the river. There was a heated enclosure that people were able to rent out that looked over the water. They sat there and took in the sunset while eating salads, fruit, and some of her other favorite snacks that he had prepared for them both.

Trina had so much fun and found herself more attracted to him than before. She was ready to jump his bones as soon as they got back in the car, but EQ had other plans. He drove them to a planetarium located on the Wayne State Campus, just in time for the 8pm show. Trina had never been to a Planetarium before and she was amazed beyond belief at the experience. As she laid back in the seat, listening to the presentation, she would steal glances at EQ and saw him so fascinated in the show that he hardly blinked. He was allowing her into his world and that turned her on even more. EQ was into the natural lifestyle. He liked talking about the planets, astrology, crystals, chakras, and he did Yoga every morning before starting his days. He was vegetarian, except when it came to conies, and loved drinking his different tea blends. It seemed like he had a blend for EVERYTHING.

Trina was amazed by the Planetarium, to then leave out the building and experience what looked like a full moon.

EQ noticed Trina looking at the moon, while opening the door for her. When he got in the car, he started talking. "It's the Full Moon in Aries tonight," he said as he started the car.

"Oh, I'm an Aries!" Trina said excitedly.

"I know ma'am, I know," EQ laughed.

"What does it mean being in Aries? I know they talked a little about it in the show tonight," Trina asked.

"It basically means that the moon's energy takes on Aries traits. With the full moon it's all about releasing energy, and things that don't work towards your goals," EQ started talking.

"And what do Aries need to release?" She asked.

He laughed. "It's not just for Aries to release, it affects everyone. But Aries is ruled by Mars and Mars rules sex and action," he said while glancing over at Trina.

Trina was already looking at him and with the 2 seconds of synchronicity, she felt her lady parts start to tingle.

"So does the moon mean that we need to release an orgasm? Cause it has been a minute for me," she laughed.

"What's a minute? Because I'm sure it's not longer than me," EQ asked.

"It don't even matter" she answered.

"Uh huh! I bet! Try 2 years!" He said.

"Two years, you haven't had sex in two-years?" Trina asked.

"Yea, when I got the Principal position, I wanted to withhold myself and just focus on my work. I also didn't really have time to date then either as I was transitioning to the position," he paused for a moment like he needed to catch his thought. "It was a hard transition and I was just getting out of a bad relationship. I was also going through my spiritual awakening, so it was best I stayed alone," he finished.

"Your spiritual awakening? How was that?" Trina asked.

"That's a conversation that could be a whole book, honestly," he laughed.

"I mean, I would love to read it the same way I'd like to…" Trina stopped herself.

"You'd like to, what?" He asked.

"I didn't mean anything. I was just talking too fast," she gave a nervous laugh.

"Well, if I'm to be honest, I would love to manifest with you and the full moon," he said while licking his lips.

"Are you trying to put a spell on me?" Trina asked with her head tilted.

EQ started laughing hysterically. "No, that's not what I mean," he started talking. "Manifesting with the moon, is somewhat like sex magic. You can bring some good things to life when you have sex on the right moon phases with the right person," he finished.

Trina couldn't believe he was so open to the conversation they were having. They had never talked about sex until this night and Trina didn't know what to think or what to say. After she was silent for an extended period of time, EQ started talking again.

"I'm sorry if I came on too strong. It's just something about you from today that I feel like we are supposed to be connected. I feel like we could do some good things together," he continued talking.

"And what's that?" Trina asked skeptically.

"Honestly, I feel like the sky's the limit. But if you ask for a million dollars, there's no doubt in my mind that we could make that happen," he said with a smile on his face.

Trina didn't know if she should be impressed or scared at this point in the conversation, but something about her wanted to fuck him even more as he talked about all his esoterical knowledge. She never had a man teach her about the moon and planets, and that stood out to her. Trina always loved to look at the moon and here he was making her fall in love with it even more.

"And how does that work?" Trina asked.

"It's called sex magic, well orgasmic manifesting," he answered before glancing over at Trina. When he saw he had her attention, he continued talking. "You know those times when you probably felt dickmatized or like someone was addicted to you?"

Trina nodded her head.

"Well, that was sex magic, it just wasn't used right," he finished.

Trina was getting intrigued as she sat up straight in her seat. "How is it supposed to be done?" She asked.

"Well, instead of thinking about how you want to be the best that person has ever had or asking who's pussy it is, you can talk life into each other. You can speak life into your goals and what you're working on for example," he answered.

"So, we are supposed to just be having sex and talking about our goals? What in the…" Trina said skeptically.

EQ started laughing. It's not exactly like that. It's basically, what you focus on when you're in ecstasy and getting ready to orgasm is what expands in your life. It's a proven fact," He said as he started scrambling through the compartment under his information dash.

As EQ grabbed for the pack of gum he was searching for, Trina pulled out her phone and looked at it for the first time since she put it on *Do Not Disturb* at their picnic. To her surprise, Damon had called her 3 times and texted her three times to match.

6:05p.m. Hey babe, what are you doing?.

An hour later:

7:10p.m. It's been a long couple of weeks and I really just want to hold you.

After no response:

8:30p.m. Are you mad at me again? I know I should've reached out to you sooner.

As soon as Trina finished reading his last message, another missed call notification popped up on her phone. It was Damon calling her again. She found herself going back and forth between if she should text him back or wait until the morning. If she texted him back, then it would be hard to keep him from coming to the house. That wasn't what Trina wanted, because she honestly wanted to fuck EQ. She decided to ignore Damon's messages and calls for the night. *I'll call him first thing in the morning,* she said to herself as she made up her mind about texting him back.

"You look like you are deep in thought," EQ said as he put a piece of gum in his mouth. "Is it my sex magic talk?" He laughed.

"Ha! No, it's not that. My friend was messaging me and I wanted to make sure everything was ok," Trina said as she put her phone back inside her bag.

"Oh, I definitely understand, and you're on a date with someone they don't know. I'm sure they want to know all the details," EQ said with a chuckle.

Trina went along with it by giving a half-smile and looking out the window as she thought about Damon calling and texting her. Not only had they not had a full conversation in almost two-weeks, he popped up like she was expected to answer whenever he called. *He got his fucking nerve!* She thought to herself as she rationalized not texting and calling him back.

It wasn't long after that EQ was pulling up to Trina's building. He pulled into a parking spot not far from the front door and shifted the gear into "park."

"I really enjoyed our time together today," EQ said with a chester cat grin on his face.

"I really liked it also, I like your attention to detail," Trina smiled.

"I'm glad you liked it!" EQ said as he shifted his body to open the door. He got out of the car and walked around to open Trina's door for her. She got out of the car and gave him a tight hug with the door wide open. While hugging, she looked up at him and closed her eyes. EQ tilted his head down and started kissing Trina while embracing her passionately. Trina pulled back from EQ and bit her bottom lip, like she was trying to preserve the little bit of lipstick she had on.

"How about a night cap?" She asked while wiping the edges of her lips of the saliva they had just exchanged.

"I would like that alot," EQ said as he walked back to the driver's side and turned the car off. Trina closed her door and started walking towards the building entrance. It was Jeffrey working the front desk that night, which wasn't normal. He usually worked days and Janet or Colby worked the nights. EQ opened the door for Trina and she led him towards the elevator.

"Have a good evening Ms. Stansby," Jeffrey said with a grin on his face. He was being messy and Trina knew it. He had seen Damon come to her condo plenty of times to know that EQ was a new visitor.

Beeeeep went the elevator as the door opened and a young couple exited the elevator before Trina & EQ got on. They rode up the elevator, in silence, staring at each other as each floor number lit up. The energy of the air screamed nervously as they both anxiously awaited what was next. They were both quiet until Trina opened the door to her home and EQ found himself in amazement. From her fireplace, to the ambiance of the space and the view of the moon, he was entranced.

"This is amazing," he said as he walked into the living room space. He swiveled his head from wall to wall taking in the art on her walls and the decor. "I love the feng shui of your living space Goddess," he said as he took a seat in front of the large window, looking out at the moon. Trina joined him on the rug, laying across as she got comfortable.

"This is my favorite spot to sit. I can sleep here for days at a time, falling asleep looking at the sky," Trina said as she turned to look at EQ. "It's like my safe space," she finished.

"I can totally see how it can do that for you," EQ said as he took his hand and started massaging her shoulders."

Trina took her hand and placed it over one of his, guiding him in the massage. "I'm going to be honest with you, before we jump into anything tonight," she said as she stopped his hand and sat up to face him.

"I have been dating someone who I am intimate with from time to time," she started before pausing.

"Is that who was texting you earlier?" He asked.

Trina nodded her head up and down. "Yea, that was him. I haven't seen him in a couple of weeks and he felt today was the perfect time for him to pop-up," she said in a lowered tone. "We aren't in a committed relationship, but I wouldn't feel right being intimate with you without the transparency," she finished as she looked down at the rug.

EQ took his hand and grabbed Trina's chin, directing her to look at him. "Look, I'm really digging you and everyday we talk, I like you more. I'm me and I could care less about another man you have in your life. What we have is magical and that's all that matters," he said as he leaned down and started kissing her passionately.

Trina immediately started feeling light-headed as she felt like they were melting into each other. As soon as she felt herself floating, he stopped kissing her and looked her in the eyes once more. "What you have with him is with him. What we have, is us and that's all I care about. Ok?" EQ asked.

"I totally understand," Trina said.

EQ immediately started rubbing the back of her neck with his hand and moved to the front. He slightly gripped her neck with one hand and took the other hand and started moving down her shirt as he laid behind her. Trina closed her eyes, awaiting what was next. The touch of his hand felt smooth like butter and he smelled like nature. He felt like home as he caressed her body from her neck down to her nipples.

"Can I have you?" EQ asked as he massaged her breasts with his arm wrapped around her neck and rubbed her womb with his other hand.

Trina grabbed his hand, that was massaging her womb, and moved it inside her panties. She started guiding him around her vagina with his hand, until his fingers were rubbing her clit and inner lips.

"Oh Goddess, you are so wet. It's like I can feel you already," EQ said as he let out a gasp.

Trina could feel his penis getting harder through his pants, the more he rubbed on her vagina. EQ started moaning in synchronicity with Trina, like he could feel what she was feeling. "You are like an aphrodisiac," EQ said as he took his hand out her pants and licked his fingers. "Can I have you?" He asked her once more.

Trina turned around, tilted her head, and said,"You already have me. Now do whatever you want."

EQ immediately rolled Trina over and sat her up. He stood up and directed her to do the same. He turned her around to face the window and walked her over to it. As he stood behind her he started undressing her under the moon. He took his time as he removed every piece of clothing from her body, kissing her skin and massaging every part of her body one move at a time. "I promise I'll be patient and take my time with you," EQ said as he removed her pants and panties.

EQ pressed Trina against the window, got on his knees and spread her ass cheeks before inviting himself into her hole. He started sucking her pussy from the back until her juices were running down her leg. He then moved his tongue up to her asshole and started rolling it around in a circle and penetrating her pussy at the same time with his three middle fingers. Trina started moaning with passion while looking out at the moon as it shone its light into her home.

"You are just as beautiful and magical as the moon," EQ said as he came up for air from tasting her. "Whatever you want in this world is yours," he finished before going back to enjoy her holes. Trina rolled her head around in a circular motion as she tried to control her orgasm. She wasn't ready to cum yet, but EQ was making it hard for her to hold it in longer.

"You are so amazing!" Trina moaned out loud as EQ started penetrating her vagina faster with his fingers.

"No, we are amazing. That's why we are here together right now," EQ said as he came up for more air. He immediately turned her around, so her back was against the window and now, he was face to face with her vagina.

"As I'm sucking on your nectar, I want you to think about all the great things you are doing now and going to do in the future. Can you do that for me, Goddess?" EQ asked as he spread her lips apart and started sucking on her clit.

"Yes baby, I can do that," Trina responded.

"I'm not your baby, I'm your King and you're a Goddess Queen. Don't you ever let someone deduce you to such," EQ said sternly.

Trina was taken aback, because no one had ever talked to her with such authority before, during sex. What took her further was the fact that she didn't feel uncomfortable. She felt empowered.

"Oh King, I love the way you motivate me. You make me feel so good," Trina said as he sucked on her clit passionately.

"It's our god energy," he said while still licking her pussy at the same time.

"Ohhhh I'm about to cum!" Trina shouted as she grabbed his head and pushed him deeper into her. "Oh King, put your finger in my ass, please?!" She begged him.

EQ obliged without questioning. He started penetrating her ass as he continued sucking on her clit. "What do you want in life, Queen? Tell me," EQ said as Trina got closer to her climax. "I want you to tell me," EQ finished.

"Oh, King. I want a family. I want to be happy with my work. I want a million dollars, I wannnnn..." Trina started before she exploded. Her creamy cum started running down and was settling on EQ's lips, mustache, and beard. He didn't stop. He kept going before stopping and saying, "You're going to get everything you desire, Queen!"

"Oh baby!" Trina said, before catching herself. "I'm sorry, King."

"You're not a sorry person, so don't ever say that word to me, ok?" EQ asked, as he stared up at her, into her eyes. "Your words have power, be careful with how you use them," he finished before grabbing both her ass cheeks and pressing his face back into her vagina lips. He started licking her like she was buttercream icing on strawberry cake. All Trina could do was lay against the window and allow herself to be overtaken by ecstasy.

EQ pleased her body from head to toe for an unknown amount of time, as they watched the moon make its way across the sky. EQ treated her like she was his Queen and he was under her command. When he finished pleasing her, he laid her down on the rug and laid down behind her. He grabbed her tight and wrapped his leg around hers making a human pretzel.

"I feel like I'm on top of the world," Trina said while looking out at the stars glistening in the night sky.

"That's because this is your world," EQ said as he kissed her on the back of the neck.

"It's something about the way you talk to me, that makes me not want you to go," Trina continued talking.

"Who said I had to?" EQ asked as he grabbed her tighter by the legs and started licking along her neck, down to the top of her back. He cupped her breasts in his hand and started massaging them softly, rolling her nipples between his finger tips.

There was a long moment of silence as EQ made sure no part of her body was left out of his royal treatment.

"What if I wanted both of you?" Trina blurted out.

EQ was silent for a moment, before rolling Trina on her back and sitting her up, as he straddled her legs around his waist, forcing them to look each other in the eyes.

"What do you mean, Queen?" He asked without taking his eyes off her. It was like he was trying to peer into her soul.

"He's a big reason why I'm in Michigan now, and I like what we have. But, honestly…" Trina started answering before pausing.

"Honestly, what?" EQ asked.

"In the perfect world, I would have both of you. You talk to a part of my soul that no man has ever done, she finished before tilting her head down to the floor.

"Don't talk to me with your head down, Goddess. I want you to always be comfortable and confident when you're talking to me," EQ said as he picked her head up.

"Honestly, what you want is normal. Monogamy has never been natural for humans, which is why it's hard," he started talking. "If you want both of us, then you can have both of us," EQ said before kissing her on the forehead.

"Are you serious?" Trina asked him, in disbelief.

"Very," EQ finished.

"Even if I wanted to marry both of you," Trina started laughing.

"Now that would be a whole other thing and level of communication. But, I'm willing to share you. You're more of a woman than what you may realize," he laughed.

Just as he got good into his laugh, there was a rattle at the front door. Trina's stomach dropped because she knew exactly what was happening. As the door started opening, EQ heard it and jolted towards the door. He was ready to jump on whoever was coming through the door, and he did just that.

"BOOM!" He clocked the unknown person across the head before Trina turned on the lights.

Just as her intuition was telling her, it was Damon. He decided that night, out of all the nights, to use his key to her home for the first time.

Trina rushed over to the door where EQ was still tussling with Damon, as he hadn't noticed who it was until Trina broke them up.

"Stop, EQ! Stop Damon!" Trina shouted out as they both straightened themselves up.

Damon looked over at EQ, half-naked, and then over to Trina who was wrapped in a thin blanket from her couch.

"So this is why you have been ignoring me? How long has this been going on?" Damon questioned.

"First, I want to know what made you just burst into my house like this without me acknowledging you!" Trina yelled at Damon.

"First off, I'm paying for this house. Second of all, you weren't answering me and I was worried," Damon responded. Trina could tell he was frustrated by the tone of his voice. She could also tell he was hurt by the slight tremble he had as he continued glancing over at EQ.

"Listen baby, we are not in a relationship, and I was already on our date when you called me," Trina started responding. She immediately got irritated and finished, " I haven't heard from you in 2 weeks!" She shouted back. "You got your nerve!"

Damon stood there quietly. It was like he had no rebuttal, but he didn't leave either.

"Listen, I can go home and let you two straighten this out," EQ said and turned to go get his shirt from the floor.

"No EQ, I need you to stay here. We need to just have this talk now," Trina said. EQ paused where he was at and turned to look Trina's way.

"Talk? What do WE need to talk about?" Damon said while looking at EQ. "I don't see what we would need to talk about," he finished.

Trina took a deep breath and let her truth out, "I want you and EQ to be my men!"

Chapter 14: Naw, I'm straight

Damon stood there looking at Trina like something was wrong with her. His face was turned up and his mouth was open like his jaw prohibited it from closing.

"What do you mean, you want both of us to be your man?" Damon asked.

"I think with good communication, we could make this work. It's not like you aren't talking to other women. I'm not stupid," she said.

Damon got quiet for a moment, "Talking to other women and sleeping with other women are two different things," he started talking. "I'm not out here putting my dick in anyone but you!" He raised his voice again.

"Aye, Man. You don't have to raise your voice at her like that," EQ said as he stepped up closer to the two.

"I wasn't talking to you, Mr. Quinn," Damon said as a way to remind him of his professional position, while looking him up and down.

EQ got quiet for a moment and started back talking. "Listen sir, I said what I said. I don't mean any harm, but you will not disrespect me."

Damon didn't even acknowledge EQ. He had his eyes fixated on Trina. He couldn't believe what was going on and couldn't decide if he should leave or beat both of their asses.

As they all stood there in silence, Trina walked over to Damon and stood in front of him. She reached out for his head and pulled him down to her. He was resisting at first, but quickly obliged to her advances. Trina started kissing Damon passionately as the blanket fell from her body. He pulled away and looked at her before looking at EQ.

"Don't worry about him baby," it's me and you right now. Trina pulled his head back and started back kissing him. Damon gave in easily and started rubbing her soft skin from her neck down to her ass. He immediately took one hand and wrapped it around her neck and started squeezing tightly as her head rolled back in ecstasy. He took his other hand and started unbuckling his pants until they fell down to his knees. The energy of the night must've secretly been turning Damon on, because his dick was as hard as a log as it stood there erect.

Trina immediately got down on her knees and started sucking his dick, while EQ was standing there watching. Damon leaned against the wall, opened his stance, closed his eyes, and started controlling Trina's head as she sucked his dick.

"Ohhhh baby," Damon said as she slurped on his magic stick. Damon took her head and pressed it all the way down on his dick, causing her to choke and a fountain of saliva started running down his dick to her breasts. "Yes, suck Daddy's dick," Damon said as Trina bobbed her head on his dick.

Damon and Trina mustn't have been paying attention to EQ, because he was down on all fours kissing Trina's ass before Damon and Trina noticed him. EQ started kissing Trina's ass cheeks before he started licking down her crack. It wasn't long until he was eating her ass, while she was sucking Damon's dick. Damon's hesitation quickly went away as Trina stopped, stood up, and started walking to the bedroom. Both Damon and EQ followed behind her like she was pulling them by an invisible rope.

Trina opened the blinds to the balcony in her room, exposing the full moon once again. She crawled on the bed, looking at her two delicious men standing at the edge of the bed. Trina laid on her back and opened her legs. Looking at Damon, she started talking again. "I want you to suck my pussy, please?" She asked him in a soft role play voice. She didn't wait for his response before turning to EQ. I want you to suck my titties and then put your dick in my mouth. I want to taste a king.

Just that fast, Trina was calling the shots and both of them did exactly what she told them to do. Damon started sucking on her pussy like he had a point to prove. It was hard for Trina to contain herself as she choked on EQ's dick. His dick was long with a curve; the type of dick that was guaranteed to always hit the g-spot. As he thrusted his dick into her mouth, EQ moaned in pleasure while talking to Trina. "You are the best to ever do this Queen!" He said as he started penetrating her mouth faster. "This is your world Goddess, tell us what to do," EQ finished talking as his legs started trembling. "Oh Queen you're about to make me cum!" EQ said loudly before taking his dick out of her mouth.

Damon wasn't phased by what they were doing. He was focused on sucking every part of her clit and lips, making it hard for her to concentrate on EQ the way she wanted to. She started squeezing her legs and pulled Damon up so he could breathe. "Take off your clothes," she said to both of them as she released Damon's face and sat up on the bed. They both stood there for a moment, before EQ started pulling his pants all the way off. When he finished, he climbed on the bed and stood over her head, facing her. EQ started kissing Trina passionately between her thighs with his Dick dangling.

While kissing, Trina took EQ's dick in her hand and lifted her body to align her pussy with his manhood. She then took his dick and started inserting it inside of her. EQ let out a loud moan as he pushed deeper inside of her. They both were moaning in unison as Damon stood there. EQ pushed deeper and deeper inside of her, allowing his curve to accommodate his passionate slow stroke. It was hard for Trina to hold in her moans as the passion was too much for her to stay quiet.

"You like that, Queen?" EQ asked while looking Trina in the eyes.

"I love it," Trina moaned back.

"I can't hear you," EQ said as he pushed all the way inside of her.

"Ahhh, I love it King, I love it!" Trina said louder as he body moved with his motions in and outside of her.

Damon walked over to the side of the bed, turned Trina's head, and put his dick in her mouth. He guided her mouth on his dick as EQ penetrated her vagina. There was moaning coming from all angles as they all found themselves falling into intimacy. Trina felt her confidence increase as she looked from

Damon to EQ. She tightened her pussy muscles so tight that EQ couldn't penetrate fully inside of her.

"Ohhh Queen, please don't deny me!" EQ moaned as he allowed his penis to roam inside of her.

"Get up real quick," Trina instructed EQ as she took Damon's penis out of her mouth. I want you to sit down, Trina said to Damon, directing him to take a seat on the bed. She sat on Damon's lap and started straddling him as she had EQ stand up over her. She immediately started sucking his dick as she bounced on Damon's dick.

Their session of ecstasy went on for at least an hour when they all experienced a joint orgasm together. The moment felt like a scene out of a movie as all three of them laid back on the bed, exhausted from the work they had just put in. Trina laid between the two with one hand on each of their dicks. She laid there stroking them up and down, giving them an extra dose of ecstasy as they found themselves moaning in sync until they both couldn't take it anymore. It was something she had only seen in porn scenes, something she never thought she'd experience in her lifetime.

Trina got warm towels and washed them both off and they laid there looking at the stars and moon.

"Sooooo, does this mean I can have both of you?" Trina broke the silence.

Damon sat up, "What do you mean both of us?" He asked.

"I want both of you to be my man," Trina said.

"I think this was better as a one-time thing," Damon snapped back. "I can't share my woman with another man."

Trina sat up to get a closer look at Damon. "But, I'm not officially your woman," she said.

He sat there quietly for a moment, contemplating on how to respond to her. "Honestly, this is something I need to think about. This is new for me," he started.

"I mean, if it makes you feel better, this is definitely new for me too," EQ jumped in.

Damon looked over at him and remained silent for a moment, before getting up from the bed. "I think I'm going to leave you two here and head home," he said as he looked around for his clothes.

Trina got off the bed and walked towards him as he made his way into the living room. She walked up behind him and wrapped her arms around his waist. "Baby, I didn't expect to fall for both of you. I really didn't," she said in a whiny voice.

"I'm sure you didn't, but this is something new to me. Especially since I got divorced because my wife was cheating on me," He responded.

Trina could hear the hurt in his voice. She had never seen him in such a vulnerable and timid mood. He was fragile.

"Is that why you haven't tried to get in a committed relationship with me?" Trina asked as she turned him to face her.

"Maybe. Little do you know, I was going to ask you to be my woman tonight," he responded.

Trina looked at him with disbelief. A part of her wanted to believe him and another part of her didn't. Damon had become so unpredictable that she didn't know what he was thinking most of the time. "Can you think about it?" She asked him.

Damon leaned down and gave Trina a kiss on the forehead. "I love you baby girl, I'll hit you up later, okay." He said as he finished zipping up his pants. He walked over towards the door, put his shirt on over his head, put his shoes on and left. There were no other words exchanged. Trina just stood there frozen from his last words to her. Damon had never told her that he loved her before and she needed to process it all. *Do I love him too?* She asked herself as she stood there looking at the door.

"Everything ok?" EQ asked, as he walked into the living room from the bedroom.

"Yea, everything is fine. He decided to go home tonight," Trina answered as she turned around to face EQ. "I really enjoyed tonight and all of the randomness it brought," she laughed.

"I agree Queen, it was definitely magical," he responded as he leaned in for a kiss.

Trina turned her head, forcing him to kiss her cheek. EQ was a little taken aback as she dodged his kiss.

"Do you want me to go home?" He asked.

"No, I want you to stay here with me tonight. I want you to hold me," she quickly answered. Still confused by what happened with Damon, Trina went to the rug and laid across it on the floor. EQ followed behind her and laid down to spoon her from the back. They didn't say anything else for the rest of the night. They just laid there looking at the moon in the sky as EQ rubbed her body.

Even though they weren't exchanging words, Trina and EQ both felt like they knew what the other was feeling. The energy was so strong that it was like they were talking more energetically than any words would be able to describe. They laid there embracing each other for the rest of the night until the sun came up. As the sun rose in the sky, Trina rolled over and kissed EQ on his forehead. He must've been a light sleeper because he woke up smiling as they were face to face.

"Good morning, Gorgeous," He said with a big grin on his face.

"Good morning, King," Trina smiled back. "Are you hungry?" She asked.

"Oh, I get good lovin' and breakfast the next morning? I guess I'm on your good side," EQ laughed as he sat up from the rug, pulling Trina towards him.

"Yesterday was amazing," Trina said as she leaned in for a kiss. She closed her eyes, took a deep breath in and went in for the kill. It felt like all of the oxygen left her body as their lips locked. All of a sudden, Trina felt a tingle in her vagina, which forced her to jump up from the rug suddenly.

"Everything okay?" EQ asked as he licked his lips.

"Yea, I'm just hungry," Trina responded while walking into the kitchen. "You eat pancakes, eggs, and breakfast potatoes?" She asked, sticking her head through the doorway.

"Yup! Just no pork, unless you want me to blow your whole house up," he laughed. Trina laughed with him and turned back into the kitchen.

It wasn't long before EQ joined Trina in the kitchen to help her prepare breakfast. They were in the kitchen playing, cooking, and enjoying each other's company like they were an old happily married couple. It was perfect. It didn't take long for Trina to forget about what happened with Damon the night before. They were both adults and the last thing she had time for was calming a grown man's feelings who only cared for hers when he wanted to.

EQ stayed over until early afternoon. It was his week for having his son, so he had to get cleaned up and pick him up that evening. EQ first told Trina about his son during the early stages of them talking. Surprisingly, Trina didn't have a problem with him having a child already. She was still unsure of if she wanted to have children, so it was slightly refreshing having a man who already had a child.

The next couple of months were great for Trina and EQ, but her relationship with Damon was non-existent. He hadn't answered her phone calls and texts, and she barely saw him at the office. It was like he was purposefully finding ways to ignore and avoid her. Even though they hadn't talked, he still made sure to pay her home payment, so he must not have been that upset at her. Meanwhile, her and EQ found themselves getting much closer in that time. One night, he asked her to be his woman and she didn't hesitate to say yes. The date was November 11th, and he made sure to make it feel special.

It was the middle of December when it seemed like life decided to go into overdrive. It was the week before the district closed for Winter Break and Trina was preparing for an outreach program at EQ's school. It was a community event they had for local middle schoolers to participate in tours and connect with high school students as mentors. Trina arrived at the school about two hours before the students were set to start arriving, to get everything set-up and in order. When she walked into the building, the first person she saw was Damon. Out of all that time and locations, she saw him at the school of her now Boyfriend.

Damon smiled as he saw Trina walk through the door. "Congratulations in advance on another successful outreach program, Ms. Stansby," he greeted her with a smile and bouquet of flowers. "I hoped I'd be able to catch you before everything started. I wanted to surprise you and tell you how proud of you I am and that I miss you," he continued. Trina gave him a half smile.

"Thank you, this was really nice of you," she responded.

"I was hoping maybe we could have dinner together this weekend? Talk over how things went." Damon asked.

"You thought coming here to ask me would be the smartest thing to do?" Trina asked.

"No, I honestly didn't think it through. I just knew I needed to see you before I lost you," he responded.

Just as Trina started to respond, EQ was coming through the doors of the building. Trina turned to greet him with a smile.

"Good morning Queen," EQ greeted Trina with a tight hug. He made sure to kiss her on the cheek and grab her ass cheek before releasing her and Damon watched it all unfold.

"Good morning King," Trina said with a big grin on her face. "I'll be in the office shortly to start getting the details together for the kids," Trina finished.

"Ok take your time, I'll get it started," EQ said before nodding and greeting Damon. "Good morning Mr. Sylvestian, I hope you are doing well today King!" He said as he reached out for a handshake.

Damon shook his hand and his face immediately changed. Trina could tell from the look on his face that he was not happy and he saw EQ as competition.

EQ went into the main office, leaving Trina and Damon to finish talking. "You and him still messing around?" Damon asked bluntly. Trina took a moment to answer him as she fished for the right words in the air. "It's a simple yes or no question," Damon continued.

"Yes, we are." Trina finally answered.

"So you're really choosing this man over me? What about all I've done for you?" He raised his voice slightly.

"Damon, you ignore and avoid me for weeks, then pop up at my work event to ask me these questions? It doesn't make sense." Trina responded with infliction in her voice.

"I woke up today and realized that I have been wrong and I'm sorry for that. I really am," Damon said.

Trina could tell from the look on his face that he was serious. This was the worst time for all of this to be happening. She still had feelings for Damon, but she loved EQ. EQ made her feel like a Queen. He taught her things and he touched her soul. Damon was an amazing provider, he was an amazing businessman, he motivated Trina to reach for more. They were both the perfect man if merged together, but she couldn't have them both.

"How about we have dinner tonight, instead of the weekend?" Trina asked. The real reason was because EQ still had his son for the week and they had plans for the weekend already, but she was interested in what he had to say.

"How's 8pm at your place?" Damon asked. "I'll order a meal to be delivered for us, to give you a chance to rest and relax," he finished.

"That sounds good," Trina responded. "I've been having a taste for Caribbean curry and jerk."

"Say no more," he said with a smile. "Have a good session, I'll see you tonight."

They gave each other a lackluster hug and Damon was on his way out the door. Trina entered the main office, and walked to the back towards EQ's office. His office was plush and zen. It was impossible to sit in his office in a bad mood. Trina took a seat in the fluffy chair in the corner, while he finished his phone call. The phone call didn't last long, because as soon as she got comfortable he was giving his attention to her.

"How was that?" He asked.

Trina already knew what he was talking about. "Oh, nothing. He wants to talk," Trina answered.

"About?" EQ asked.

"I really don't know, but we are going to talk about it over dinner tonight," she responded.

"Well thank you for at least letting me know," EQ said as he turned to face his computer screen. It was obvious that he felt a type of way.

"I mean, I could've easily lied about it," she responded.

EQ was silent for a moment. "So what are you going to do when he tells you that he loves you and wants you back in his life?"

"Whoa, whoa, I think we are jumping the gun," Trina pleaded.

"No, I'm just a man and I know how some of us operate," he continued. "You still want him?" EQ asked.

Trina was silent for a moment. "He's a big reason why I'm here and he's still paying my $2000 a month house bill, I can at least see what he has to say E!" Trina raised her voice.

"I mean, you did say that you wanted two men. I can't be mad at it I guess…" EQ responded while typing heavily on his computer.

"Look, let's talk about this later. We have a long day ahead of us and I don't want us to get off track," Trina changed the conversation.

EQ raised his eyebrow before turning to face his computer again. It was obvious that he had a slight attitude, but Trina was in no position to try and fix it. The students would be there in a little over an hour and she still had work to do. They barely talked to each other the rest of the time she was in his office. They exchanged a few words here and there when one of them had a question about the logistics of the program. That was all.

The program went perfectly and she was sure no one could tell that there was bad energy between her and EQ. They both played their feelings off well and made sure to keep their professionalism top notch in front of the kids. None of their co-workers knew they were dating and Trina wasn't ready for the cat to be out of the bag yet either. The last thing they needed was to bring their lover's quarrel to work.

Chapter 15: TF is love really?

That night, Damon showed up at her house at exactly 8pm and the food followed behind him by a few minutes. One thing about Damon, whenever he said he was going to do something, he did it and it was always clutch. He didn't even have time to take his shoes off before having to meet the delivery person at the front desk. When he walked back into her home with the food, Trina instantly felt her stomach and heart smile. She had been craving Caribbean food and that was the perfect time to finally indulge.

Damon helped Trina get the food fixed up on plates and set on the table. He even brought candles with holders to set the mood for a candlelight dinner. Trina could already tell where the night was headed, she just didn't know how to walk around it.

"Thank you for agreeing to meet with me," Damon said as he pulled out her favorite wine and two classes from her cabinet.

"Of course. It would be wrong of me to not hear you out," Trina responded.

"You know, I've been thinking alot about you and what you asked me the last time we talked," Damon started talking. He wasted no time ripping the bandaid off their scars. "How would it even look if we did that?" He asked.

"What part are you talking about?" Trina asked. "We talked about alot of things," she finished.

"The part about having both Mr. Quinn and myself," he answered with no hesitation.

Trina was quiet for a moment. She hadn't prepared for the conversation even though she knew in her heart that it would come up. For once, she was ill-prepared for something, yet she wasn't nervous.

"I really don't know, I have never done it before," she responded. "I guess we would have to have guidelines on boundaries."

Damon played with his food for a moment, as if he was going to find the right words in his rice and peas. "I think I could do it, if I understood how it would look," he started talking. "This time away from you made me miss you even more and honestly, I don't want to lose you Trina," Damon said with conviction. "You make me want to experience life. When I'm with you I feel like my cares of the world leave. The stress I have is removed," he continued. "When I didn't contact you for those 2 weeks, it was honestly because I was falling hard for you and didn't know how to handle it. Then to find that you were feeling someone else, that almost crushed me," he finished.

Damon looked up at Trina to analyze the look on her face. He was looking for an answer, but Trina kept a straight face.

"There are alot of things that I loved about us and things that I wish were better. I do feel you show me another side of life that I respect wholeheartedly, but you can't just disappear whenever you can't handle something. That's not fair to me," Trina responded.

Damon was quiet for what felt like 20 minutes, but was really only like 25 seconds. "Listen Trina, I've let you see a side of me that not everyone gets a chance to see. You're supposed to be in my life and I'm not letting you go!" Damon said with great confidence. It's like he took a sip of the confidence juice from Space Jam because he was talking like a whole different person from a short while before.

"You know I'd need to talk to him about it, right?" Trina asked.

"So are you saying he was never ok with it?" Damon asked.

"What I'm saying is that I don't know if he feels the same way that he felt a couple of months ago," she responded.

"Well, in the case he says no, can I have you one more time?" Damon asked. "I need you Trina," he pleaded.

Trina couldn't lie, she missed having hardcore sex with Damon. EQ was a sensual lover. They made love, but her and Damon knew how to fuck. He knew how to take her all the way down and bring her back up again. They both brought her ecstasy but in different ways.

"I'm in a relationship," Trina answered.

"With all due respect baby, fuck that relationship," Damon raised his voice. "You were mine before him and I promise you will be mine if he leaves," Damon continued.

It was his confidence, for Trina. For some reason the toxicity of the conversation was starting to make her vagina wet. She wanted to tell him to fuck her over the couch raw and hard, but she couldn't do that type of thing without thinking about EQ.

"Baby, as much as I would love to have you lean me over the couch, you know I can't do that to him," Trina asserted as she shifted in her seat.

Damon could sense that she wanted him just as much as he wanted her. He knew he had to have her and he was determined to have her. Trina could tell from the look in his eyes that he wasn't going to give up. She knew as soon as he bit his bottom lip that she was going to lose to her pussy. Her pussy was starting to take over and she was holding on by a thread as she listened to the rumbling of his voice.

"Listen, we don't have to fuck, I just want to taste you. Your cum makes me feel like a superhero," Damon said as he stood up from the couch.

Trina took another bite of her food as she attempted to act like she didn't know what he was doing. Damon made his way over to her, got on his knees and started kissing her thighs that were exposed from her dress. He started rubbing her thighs and moving his hands up towards the inside.

"You can tell me to stop if you want to. I promise I will," Damon said in his sexy voice.

The thing is, he knew it was hard for Trina to resist him once she got that close to him. He knew he had won already. There was no way Trina was going to deny him.

"Do you want me to stop?" Damon asked as his hands reached the inside of her thighs, touching the outside of her pussy lips through her panties.

Trina moaned from his touch and Damon took that as a no. He continued his conquest of kissing her and moved his way upwards as he pulled her panties down at the same time.

"Did you miss daddy?" He asked as she stopped at the entrance to her pussy gates.

Trina moaned, "Yes daddy, I missed you."

"I know you did," Damon said cockily. "You've been giving my pussy away and I don't know how I feel about that," he continued.

Trina leaned back in her chair, giving him easier access to her pussy gate. They both already knew what was coming, Trina was simply bracing herself for the impact.

Damon wasted no time, once he spread her lips open his tongue was inside her pussy in a matter of seconds. Somehow he was sticking his tongue inside her vagina while sucking her clit at the same time. As much as she tried to conceal it, her moans got louder.

"Alexa, turn on smooth jazz!" Trina moaned out to her Alexa device.

The vibes were set, she was wet, and she had her man back. Nothing else mattered in that moment. Damon still knew how to please her and she made sure to leave no cum inside of her as she found herself squirting in his face. He pulled back, licking it off his face.

"I knew you missed me," he said with a cocky look on his face. "Now come ride me and show me how much you missed daddy," he said as he walked over to the couch unzipping and pulling down his pants as he walked.

Trina had no objections and did just as he said like she was under some type of spell. All of the hesitation she previously had went out the door.

When she got on top of him, there was no stopping. From fast to slow, she rode him passionately as he moaned and controlled her body by grasping her waist while sucking her neck and breasts.

"Our bodies were made for each other," Damon said as he thrusted his manmade inside of her, while she straddled him. Trina let out a loud passionate moan. "You like when daddy go deep, don't you?" He asked her before grabbing her face and kissing her. "If I can't have you, no one can have you," Damon said as he looked deep into her eyes.

Trina closed her eyes and rolled her head backwards. Damon grabbed her head and forced her to look at him again. "I'm serious, Trina. I'm not letting you go," he finished. "We were made for each other."

Trina knew in her heart that he was serious, but she didn't take it too seriously. People say all types of things while having sex.

"As long as you don't give my dick to no one else," she responded.

"If I ever get the desire to put it somewhere else, I'll make sure you're there with me," he said while fucking her faster.

Trina closed her eyes and allowed the moment to continue as it was. When she came back to reality, she squatted on his dick with her feet planted on each side of him. As she started bouncing and grasping his dick, faster and faster, she could tell he was ready to cum. Instead of pulling her off him like he always did, he grabbed her waist and started fucking her back.

Trina started moaning uncontrollably as she embraced the pleasure and pain he was creating inside of her. He didn't stop either. Next thing she knew, he stopped pumping her and gave her a huge bear hug. She immediately wiggled from his grip and jumped up, analyzing her pussy. "Did you just cum inside of me?" She asked him.

"We always do, I didn't think it would be any different this time." He answered.

"Yea, I also gave you permission before we ever went that far. You don't know if I'm ovulating or anything," Trina said as she ran to the bathroom. She immediately forced herself to pee and started wiping her vagina down with soap and water.

"I'm sorry baby, I didn't think anything of it, I promise," Damon pleaded as made it to the bathroom doorway.

"Yea, ok Damon," she responded. She didn't believe him and he knew she didn't.

"Are you ovulating?" He asked.

"No, I don't think I am. It's just the principle of it all!" Trina shot back.

Damon's face turned to a view of gloom. He knew at that moment that he had fucked up miserably, in a moment that he was trying to make up for past transgressions. "I promise I'm sorry, I can go get a Plan B," he offered.

"Cool, now I'm a hoe looking for $40!" Trina said angrily. "I'll be ok," she continued.

"Can I please make it up to you?" He asked.

"I need some time to think Damon, this has become too much," she responded. "It might be best if you left," she finished. "I'll give you a call tomorrow after I've had the chance to think through all of this.

As soon as she finished talking, she heard her phone ringing in the other room. She already knew who it was. EQ knew she was meeting with Damon, so that was his check-in call to see how it was going. The phone continuously rang as if he was calling back to back with no break between.

"Do you want me to grab that for you?" Damon asked.

"Please?" She replied.

Damon brought her phone back and it was still ringing.

"Hey King," she answered the phone.

"Hey Queen, how is it going?" He asked.

"It's going fine, he's getting ready to leave now, can I call you back in a few while I clean up?" Trina responded.

EQ paused for a moment before agreeing to her calling him back. They ended the call and Trina found herself in emotional shambles. For the first time since everything had started, she didn't know what she wanted nor did she know how she should handle it all.

"Is it ok if I call you in the morning?" Damon asked.

"I'll call you," Trina reiterated.

"Touche'" Damon responded as he turned to get dressed. It took him a good five minutes to get his clothes and leftovers situated before he returned to the bathroom to give Trina a kiss. He went in for her mouth but she turned her head so fast he caught her cheek. He turned to leave and nothing else was said.

Just as Damon left the house, Trina's phone started ringing again. She thought it was EQ calling her cause she was taking too long, but to her surprise, it was Kisha. Trina couldn't believe her eyes as she let the phone ring again before answering. She hadn't talked to Kisha since before she left San Francisco and she missed her homegirl so much.

"Hello," Trina answered the phone.

"Hey girl, I know it's late there, do you have a few minutes to talk?" Kisha asked.

"Of course I do," Trina quickly responded.

"I just wanted to say that I'm so sorry for how everything went down when you were preparing to move. I should've never treated you like that, you didn't deserve it. I was your friend and I should've been there to support you and your transition," Kisha started apologizing like word vomit. "So much happened that weekend and I took it out on everyone. It's no excuse, but I feel like God has been torturing me ever since," she continued.

Trina immediately stopped thinking about her problems and was tuned into Kisha. "You know I forgive you love. You're my girl. What was going on that you couldn't tell me?" Trina asked.

Kisha took in a deep breath, before responding. "So, you know how we went on that quick family camping trip that weekend of your conference?" Kisha asked with a lowered tone. Trina hadn't heard Kisha sound like that since the day she found out she was pregnant.

"Yup! You were so excited to be getting away for the weekend," Trina responded.

"Well, it was all good until I found out that my life was a lie," Kisha said before bursting into tears.

"What happened?" Trina asked, concerned for her best friend.

"I found out that Kev got another woman pregnant," Kisha said through the tears. "He had been cheating on me the whole time," she fought through the tears. "I'm so sorry for treating you the way I did, I was in a dark place," she finished.

"Girl, you know I'm still here and I'm going to be here as you get through this," Trina assured Kisha.

Kisha started sniffling as she blew her nose, "Well, that's not the only reason why I called you. I wanted to apologize and see how my bestie was doing. I miss you so much!" Kisha said, trying to get more excited.

"Girl, so much has been happening in my life, I don't even know where to start…" Trina responded.

"Well how about the beginning. I have time as long as you do," Kisha reassured her.

And this is when shit started to get real.....

ABOUT THE AUTHOR

Nina Monroe, also known as Moe Nicole, has always had a vivid imagination that never seemed to fit mainstream.

Both Of Em': Volume 1 is the first of a series of books outlining the journey of a Black millennial woman in the public sector. The series is based off a mixture of stories, ideas she has had, and experience with various cultures.

This is Moe's 4th print book and she is excited for the other books to come after. This is her 2nd non-fiction novel and 1st erotica novel of many to come. I hope you enjoyed the read!

Checkout my other books!

Acknowledgments

To those who have always believed in me, supported me, and motivated me when I was down. I will forever send love and positive vibes your way. Thank you for letting me be me without judgment. May you have all your heart desires, Pooh!